W

A Royal Summer of Love

Jenny felt astonished that the other two women could have been so much impressed by the Earl's passing interest in her that they should feel it necessary to greet her so coldly. Did they really believe themselves in danger of losing him to a peasant girl?

They had no need to worry. Away from him, and led into the first dance by John Morley, she armed herself anew. She must be on her guard against letting a dream carry her away. The Earl was not for her. Desirable, charming and even admirable he might be, but she could desire and admire only from a distance. For the summer would end, and with it her small part in his world. She must not covet anything she found there—even love.

Bantam Circle of Love Romances
Ask your bookseller for the books you have missed

Dear Friend,

Enter the Circle of Love—and travel to faraway places with romantic heroes . . .

We read hundreds of novels and, each month, select the very best—from the finest writers around the world—to bring you these wonderful love stories . . . stories that let *you* share in a variety of beautiful romantic experiences.

With Circle of Love Romances, you treat yourself to a romantic holiday—anytime, anywhere. And because we want to please you, won't you write and let us know your comments and suggestions?

Meanwhile, welcome to the Circle of Love— we don't think you'll ever want to leave!

Best,
Cathy Camhy
Editor

CIRCLE OF LOVE

The Cinderella Season

Elaine Daniel

BANTAM BOOKS
TORONTO · NEW YORK · LONDON · SYDNEY

THE CINDERELLA SEASON

A Bantam Book/published by arrangement with
Robert Hale, Ltd.

PRINTING HISTORY

Published by Robert Hale Limited, London

CIRCLE OF LOVE, the garland and the ring designs
are trademarks of Bantam Books, Inc.

Bantam edition/April 1982

ISBN 0-553-21503-5

Published simultaneously in the United States and Canada

Bantam Books are published by Bantam Books, Inc. Its
trademark, consisting of the words "Bantam Books" and the
portrayal of a rooster, is Registered in U.S. Patent and
Trademark Office and in other countries. Marca Registrada.
Bantam Books, Inc., 666 Fifth Avenue, New York, New York
10103.

PRINTED IN THE UNITED STATES OF AMERICA

0 9 8 7 6 5 4 3 2 1

One

At first it seemed a day no different from all the rest. Jenny waited until her mother had gone to work before she got up. She enjoyed the silence of the empty house, and the self-indulgence of a lazy breakfast—and besides, there was nothing else to do. The housework never took long, and there wasn't any shopping, she had been into town yesterday. So it was as well to make the small incidents of the morning last as long as they would.

Outside, the air was hazy, the lawn still misted with dew. Daffodils hung their heads motionless over the grass beneath the apple tree, and in among the branches a blackbird sang. Nice to be a blackbird, Jenny thought, standing by the kitchen window to watch him. His song was his reason for existing; nobody expected anything more from him, nobody stood behind him pushing him out into the world, urging him to make a career or to settle for any job that was going. He had been born to sing, and that was what he did, and it was enough.

Perhaps she wasn't being strictly fair. Her mother

Elaine Daniel

didn't push or grumble any more than was perfectly reasonable in the circumstances. Jenny had left college in the summer, and it was now Easter of the following year and still she had no job. It wasn't that she hadn't tried; she had gone after all sorts of openings—commercial design, book jackets, fashion illustration—but the answer was always the same. They didn't want a highly qualified art historian, they wanted a straightforward illustrator, and preferably one with practical experience. Theory was no good to them, however well she might draw. And times were hard and the market depressed; it wasn't the moment for selling expertise in a practically non-existent field.

Her mother tried not to complain. But, almost annoyingly self-sufficient since the death of her husband—Jenny's father—two years before, she tended to lecture.

"I'm pleased to have you about the house and to have all the chores taken care of," she had said. "It's the greatest luxury to come home every evening to a spotless home. But I'm worried about your future. You can't make a career of housework, can you? You'll get stale and dispirited and end up losing even the urge to break free—I can remember the feeling so well from when you were small and I was at home all day. It's thoroughly depressing."

The housebound blues, in fact. Jenny was learning all about them. One day followed on so very much like the last in a gentle, deadly monotony, and there was never any urgency or excitement in anything one did. Gradually even the hope of change seemed to die. Jenny had begun to lose faith in her ability ever to break free and to make her own way in the world.

This morning a letter lay on the kitchen table. Waiting for the toast to be done she ran a knife under the flap and opened it, knowing already from the handwriting on the envelope that it was nothing so unexpected or exciting as the offer of a job, but only a letter from Clare.

"Jenny, love," she read, "are you still marooned at home? I ought not to hope so—I ought to be wishing you gloriously restoring Holbeins and Turners for the National Gallery, but the thing is that I'm selfish and I want you here instead. What do you say to this?

"As you know, my Pa looks after the Langton horses. This means that during the season, when the Castle is open to the public, families on the estate rally round to work as guides and keepers and things—you know what I mean, here is the actual Dresden chamberpot in which the fifth Countess hid her diamonds at the time of the great Onion Rebellion in eighteen forty-six, that kind of patter, very easy to learn. I've never been here for the whole season before, but this year I was offered the Print Room, which is a hotch-potch collection of engravings, water-colours, books and things—some lovely stuff, but a bit academic and therefore not the busiest of the public rooms. I suppose that's why they gave it to me. I was to have paired with a woman who's done it before, but at the last minute she's had to

3

rush off to her sister in Canada who's having a baby and trouble with her husband. And this is where you come in. I told Edward about you (he organises it all, and is really rather special) and he said you sounded just the person. So are you interested?

"You know what I expect you to answer. Really, the work's not exacting and the pay is good—and there's the added pleasure of being with the most charming people. Even the visitors aren't too bad. You'd live with us, of course—in fact I was going to ask you to come just for a visit, only this would be so much more fun, wouldn't it? Do say you'll come. There's no need for anything formal; I can let Edward know, and everything else can be arranged when you get here. Tradition demands that you sign a funny sort of mediaeval declaration of allegiance to the Family, but that won't bother you, will it? Certainly it wouldn't if you'd ever met the Earl, who's the kind of man one would take any oath for. Besides, it's not really like the middle ages, when one might have had to march off and actually fight for them.

"Ring me, will you, and put me out of my suspense? Or write if you'd rather, but write *soon*. There's so much I want to tell you, and so much to show—you absolutely must come, Jenny. It would be such a perfect summer."

Jenny had to read the letter through twice before its message went home. Then she let it drop onto the kitchen table and sat down abruptly, her legs suddenly too weak to hold her. Sun had broken through the haze beyond the window. In the apple tree the blackbird sang as though his heart might burst from happiness.

It was much too good to be true. Of all the people in the world Clare was the one she felt closest to. They had gone through college together, and somehow it had never mattered in the least that Clare came from a wealthy family and Jenny did not; they had shared so many dreams, so much laughter and despair and hope. But then it had all ended, Clare going back to her privileged life on the Langton estate and Jenny setting about the business of trying to put her art training to practical use in a world that wasn't much impressed by it. College life had been an interlude, very pleasant while it had lasted, but not like the real thing. Reality could be very drab.

All the same they had corresponded regularly. Clare's letters were always full of delight in the life she led—Hunt balls, riding, parties, the comings and goings of the Langton family. Jenny had been driven to contrive news, small details of the daily round made to sound as amusing as she could make them, accounts of abortive interviews for jobs, descriptions of her regular pilgrimage to the Labour Exchange. Clare had never encountered any of these things, yet somehow Jenny could not resent that fact. And now, to spend a summer in Clare's world, and to get paid for it, was the most marvellous thing imaginable.

She sat quite still until the pounding of her heart had subsided. What exactly did the letter say?

Engravings, water-colours, books—and Langton Castle, of course, that fairy-tale place she had never seen and yet knew so well from Clare's descriptions. There would be gardens and woods and fields, a country life of dogs and horses, and even the leisure to enjoy them. There would be other people who liked the sort of things she loved. And she would have the freedom of the Langton collection, that incredible gallery of paintings reckoned to be among the best and most valuable in the world.

She felt quite sick with excitement, and with an unreasonable apprehension in case somehow it should turn out not to be true. But the letter was there, real and undeniable—black ink on grey paper, with an engraved heading: Morleys, Langton Castle, Leicestershire. Unless Clare were the victim of some quite unprecedented brain storm, that was where Jenny would be spending the summer.

She had no doubt that her mother would be both delighted and relieved. Much as she might try to disguise her feelings, there was no doubt that it depressed and irritated her to have Jenny unemployed and aimless about the house. Her own career absorbed her, it was the mainspring of the life she had built up after her divorce. Jenny no longer belonged at home with her. So it would be good for both of them, this summer at Langton. And afterwards—who knew?—all kinds of opportunities might arise when she could claim that she had worked for the Earl of Langton. People were impressed by titles. British society might have changed a great deal, but there were pockets of resistance still; the nobility still represented something, especially when backed by the kind of wealth the Langtons possessed.

There, of course, lay the fly in the ointment. Clare's family were well off, but not so disproportionately rich that Jenny had ever felt it necessary to disapprove of them. Clearly they were nice people and they worked for their living. Not so the Langtons. Such wealth as theirs had been accumulated over the centuries, built up from the acquisition of land and the exploitation of people. They lived, now, on the fortunes of former times; they married money, used money to make more. They were privileged and idle beyond what ought to be allowed in a fair society. Jenny, who knew only too well what a struggle life could be, found it impossible to imagine that she would ever like the Langtons. She resented them; she saw a desperate ugliness in the fact that they could live in Langton Castle or their house at Tathwell, or in London, when other families had to fight to keep up even one home, and some had not so much as that. She could not believe that any one person had a right to all that the Earl of Langton owned. And so to work for him would be to betray her principles. She would be selling herself to the enemy.

For a little while it really troubled her. But then she reflected that after all she would be making a convenience of Lord Langton and his castle. It was he who would be serving her ends. In employing her for the summer he was at least putting a tiny fraction of his ill-gotten wealth to a useful purpose. And so she might retain her principles and still do what she wanted, which was very satisfactory. Moreover she need not hurt Clare's feelings by a refusal, and that was better still.

After her mother had come home that night and had been told the good news, she rang Clare. All was arranged.

"I was sure you would," said Clare. "It's a job tailor-made for the two of us. And Langton's so lovely in the summer, I couldn't bear for you not to see it. The park's full of daffodils just now, so beautiful they make me giddy. Oh, and people come and go, everything's alive and interesting—I've so much to tell you, Jenny, things I couldn't possibly write down. You have to come and share them."

There was a convenient train, it transpired, which would take Jenny from Oxford to Leicester, where she would be met and conveyed to Langton in time for lunch.

"Don't worry about bringing vast heaps of clothes," Clare instructed her. "You can always borrow from me. But you'll need one ball gown, for the Daffodil Ball, you know, at the castle. Otherwise it's tee shirts, jeans, and a sober dress or two for work. Oh, and a swimsuit, because we use the castle pool when They aren't here."

It was quite funny, Jenny thought, the way the Langtons seemed to be spoken of in capitals—They, the Family, as if they were on a par with the Deity. She wondered whether even she might eventually acquire the habit. In the enclosed world of their own estates no doubt they were royalty of a kind, but she hoped that she would be able to resist them. She had no intention of being dazzled.

Her mother drove her into Oxford on the appointed day. Jenny found a window seat on the train, anxious to see all that she could, because Clare had explained that the line passed not far from Langton Castle on its way into Leicester. One could see the castle on the summit of a hill; it was a famous view, and not on any account to be missed.

At the last moment her mother became anxious.

"Promise me that you'll come home again if it doesn't suit," she insisted. "One really doesn't know what these people may be like. The Langtons, I mean, not Clare's family, I'm sure they're charming. But the Langtons—"

"What about them?" asked Jenny, amused.

"Oh, well—they're a rackety crowd, I wouldn't wonder. I dare say the gossip columns invent a great deal, but not all of it."

"I think I can cope," said Jenny. "I don't imagine that the wicked Earl is exactly waiting to sweep me off my feet and into a life of Sin."

"No, but—oh, Jenny, I don't want to feel that I've rushed you into anything, just because I've been anxious for you to start on a career. You have to let me worry, you know. It's a mother's prerogative."

The station blurred as the train slid slowly out. Suddenly Jenny wanted a little longer to make up her mind, to be sure that it wasn't after all safer to stay at home, where at least boredom was familiar and secure. But she had left it too late for questions.

Her mother's fears were momentary, no more, the effect of parting; in the natural order of things they ought to have come sooner, that was all. Jenny had been already too long at home.

The train went into a tunnel, and Jenny could see her reflection in the window. Her face was a pale oval, the eyes dark smudges, her shiny dark hair straight and faintly swinging with the movement of the train. How was she going to look against the background of Clare's sort of life? There was no way she could hope to rival Clare's extravagant blonde beauty; her own style was altogether quieter. But she hoped that she might fit in by virtue of being so very unremarkable. There wasn't a great deal about her to which anyone could take exception. Provided she kept her views on the Langtons' wealth and titles to herself she might pass the summer very comfortably.

The journey was uneventful. There was no mistaking Langton Castle when it came; like a great outcrop of rock it crowned the hill, stone bleached by the spring sunlight, trees crowding thick around and under it. On every side the country stretched clean and unspoiled, smaller hills gently subsiding into a fertile plain upon which, here and there, grey stone farms and hamlets were set pleasantly as if they had been put there on purpose to enhance the view. The Vale of Langton, it was called. And every acre belonged to the Family.

She watched the castle for as long as she could see it, until the angle of the train hid it from her. Then very soon the countryside gave way to raw brick suburbs and then to the grime and confusion of Leicester. Clare and her brother John were waiting there on the platform.

Amid all the scurrying and noise of the station Clare flung her arms round Jenny and hugged her.

"Oh, I am so glad and relieved to see you! I was sure something would have turned up at the last minute to prevent your coming, it seemed so much too good to be true. You haven't ever met John, have you? John, this is Jenny at last."

"Hello, Jenny-at-last." He was tall and tanned, with an engaging openness of manner and the somehow understated, almost casual good looks of the well-bred Englishman. It would have been impossible not to like him at sight.

"You might have known that wild horses wouldn't have kept me back," she said to them both. "And I looked out for Langton, and I think it's absolutely beautiful. I can't wait to get there."

"Let's take your cases, then," said Clare, "and get away from this noisy station and back to Langton as quickly as we can."

Between them they humped her luggage to the barrier and out to where the car was waiting, and all the way they kept up a disjointed conversation, shouting over the roar of diesel engines going at full blast.

The quiet of the car was almost like being deaf. It was a large saloon with deep, leather upholstered seats and a silky engine. John drove so that Clare and Jenny could sit in the back and talk, which they did incessantly all the way to Langton.

"The Family are due at any moment," Clare said at one point. "They mean to stay a week or so and then go on to Tathwell, which is where they mainly live when the castle's open—though He spends a little more time at the castle because of having to run things."

"Ah, yes," said Jenny gravely. "He must have a great deal to do, poor man."

Clare shot her a look of suspicion.

"Well, so he does," she declared. "He likes to see to everything himself. You'd be amazed at all there is to the administration of an estate like Langton. And ultimately the responsibility falls on him."

"Oh, I'm sure. Who else is there in the Family?" Even when she said it the word came out with a capital letter. How was one to prevent it?

"There's the Dowager Countess," said Clare. "And Rowena—the Lady Rowena, that is."

"She being the Earl's wife?"

"Oh, no. His sister. He's not married."

"Ah." She looked sidelong at Clare, wondering if perhaps her reverence for the Family might spring from a personal interest in this unmarried Earl. It would be like Clare, to fall extravagantly in love with the nearest thing to a fairy-tale prince she could find conveniently to hand. But there was something about an Earl that discouragingly suggested desiccation—mutton-chop whiskers and moth-eaten ermine. She could not imagine this in any very romantic light, and especially in connection with any creature so glowingly pretty and full of life as Clare.

John Morley drove very smoothly. Surprisingly soon they were out of Leicester and threading their way neatly through winding by-roads towards Langton. Jenny watched the hill grow bigger as they gradually approached it.

"How old is the castle?" she asked Clare. "I know nothing about it beyond what you've told me, and somehow that's a bit scrappy."

"My mind being such a rag bag," agreed Clare. "It was built on a Norman site, but actually it's a terrible eighteenth century fake, if you take that point of view, or a glorious eighteenth century realisation of the Gothic style if you don't. It's vast, that's the most noticeable thing about it. And the gardens are utterly lovely."

Jenny thought of her mother's small suburban patch of lawn, the daffodils and the apple tree. But then at least the Langtons opened their gardens to the public so that, for a price, anyone might enjoy them.

"How long have they been opening the castle?" she wanted to know.

"This is the fifth year. It was after old Lord Langton died. He would never have permitted it, but the present Earl believes one should."

"Bully for the present Earl." No doubt it assuaged his feelings of guilt, thought Jenny. Even an Earl must be aware that times were changing. Better to change with them than to be overtaken by events and forced into capitulation.

The road now began to wind through dense trees towards the summit of the hill, turning around and back on itself against the steepness of the slope. The castle was hidden by dark branches. Presently they came to high gates, magnificently wrought in iron and gilded, set into a thick wall of grey stone. There was a lodge, and as the car drew up at the gates a woman came out to open them.

"Morning, Mr. John. Lovely day again."

"It is indeed. Thank you, Mrs. Dawson."

The gates swung wide and the car slid between them into the massive gloom of a thick wood. A long drive continued to wind its way up the hillside, which grew ever steeper. Great banks of shiny rhododendron flanked the roadway, and beyond them trees cut out any view save that of the sky. It was like being in some strange time tunnel, cut off from the world, eerie and unnerving. Here and there a pathway led into the bushes and Jenny caught a glimpse of wooded hillside sloping away, but apart from such small paths it was the most private place imaginable.

At last the trees gave way to a huge wall on one side, and the drive made one more turn and then came out with breath-taking suddenness onto a gravelled, open plateau. There, like a great Gothic wedding cake, stood the castle, serene above the treetops, gazing into the distance over an infinite blue vista of vale and hills. A broad terrace surrounded it, with balustrades and gun emplacements, and then the garden dropped away in a series of giant steps, enchanting, green and blossomy. Jenny gazed about her and behind her as the car swept under the towering walls, gliding round the castle and past a small city of stable yards, kitchen gardens, greenhouses and other buildings, and on down a sloping, curving drive towards a grey rectangle of stone house and stables some little way down an open, grassy park.

"That's us," said Clare contentedly. "Morleys—named long before we came there, which is a coincidence, don't you think? It's a nice place."

"It's beautiful." Jenny looked back at the great pile of the castle shining in the sun, and then again at the stone buildings of Morleys before her. It was more splendid, more beautiful than anything she could have imagined. There had to be a catch somewhere. It wasn't like real life to be so generous, and she would not dare to believe in her good fortune until it had given her abundant proof that it was genuine. She half expected to wake up at any minute.

Two

The Morley parents proved to be every bit as charming as their children. Jenny had wondered if they might constitute the fly in the ointment, but they were warm and welcoming and entirely delightful. Clare had got her beauty from her mother; Mrs. Morley had the same vitality, the same joy in living as her daughter, but it was restrained by maturity and made her seem somehow a very strong, very capable person. Leonard Morley was a man of more diffident charm, quiet, and yet authoritative. One would always listen when he chose to speak. He fitted well into the setting of his home, which was furnished with the kind of casual, almost haphazard juxtaposition of things which miraculously blended though they did not in the least look as though they had been chosen with that end in mind. There was nothing contrived about the house, Jenny thought; it seemed rather to have grown according to some design of nature. The pictures on the walls were meant to be lived with; the carpets were a fine muddle of reds and blues, old, beautiful things whose richness was somehow increased by use and age.

Her room had a dormer window and a view of the castle.

"I thought you'd rather," said Clare. "You could have had a bigger room on the other side, but I thought you'd like to see the castle."

"Oh, I do. It's a perfect room!"

The walls were papered with pale lavender stripes so faint that they hardly showed. There was a blue carpet with an Afghan rug over it, and the bedspread and curtains were patchwork, rectangles of blue and rose and white. A writing desk stood under the window, pale grey Langton notepaper on it, and there were bookshelves and two armchairs covered in a striped fabric similar to the paper on the walls.

It felt like home at once.

"My room's next door," Clare told her. "And across the landing there's a little pantry—for things like hot water bottles, you know, and midnight cocoa. John and Mummy and Daddy sleep on the other side of the stairs, so we're practically self-contained. We even share our own bathroom."

"Like college again, only better."

"Heaps better! College was so scruffy, and this is beautiful. I love Langton, Jenny—I want to be here for ever. I don't ever want to have to go away or do anything else." For a moment Clare's voice was desolate. Jenny looked at her in surprise.

"Need you, then?" she asked.

"Well—oh, I hope not. If only all goes well. But—"

There was the distant, muffled sound of a gong. Vexed, Clare shook her head, and whatever confidence had been about to come was lost.

"I'll tell you later," she said, leaving Jenny to speculate as to whether the Earl himself might not have something to do with the matter. Awkward, for a daughter of one of his employees to fall in love with the titled gentleman.

Luncheon was a pleasant meal, informal yet unhurried. They sat in a room whose windows looked out over the sloping park down into the valley. Off to one side Jenny could see a large, level meadow railed off and set up with training jumps for horses.

"We breed and train mostly show-jumpers," Leonard Morley told her, catching the direction of her gaze. "Some of the best in the world are ours. Two were jumped in the last Olympics."

"I ought to confess now, I suppose," said Jenny. "I never sat on a horse in my life. I just about know which end is which, and that's all."

"Then you couldn't have come to a better place," Clare's mother declared. "We'll have you jumping before the end of the summer. She could begin on Max, don't you think, Clare?"

"Max is our old faithful, and you couldn't fall off him if you tried," Clare explained.

"Just you watch me." But Jenny was thrilled. It seemed so long since she had ever done anything really new. All the interesting learning seemed to happen when one was young, and then to stop, leaving an ill-defined hunger which one had no idea how to appease. She felt, now, that she had always wanted to ride without knowing that she wanted it, and she meant to learn fast and to do it well.

After luncheon Clare wanted to show her the castle.

"A few people may be about—we opened officially last week, but since it's a weekday and early in the season I don't suppose there'll be crowds."

"Are you not working?" Jenny asked her.

"Not today. Edward—that's Mr. Channing, the steward—he offered to do it for me so I could meet you and show you around." Clare's cheeks were suddenly very pink. Not the Earl, then, thought Jenny. Edward Channing. Well, it was a promising sort of name.

"He's the one you said was rather special, isn't he?" she commented. "What's he like, then?"

They were strolling along the drive which led up the hill to the castle. Birdsong was a thick, sweet haze all about them, and the sun felt warm on their faces. Jenny thought she had never breathed air so fragrant and fresh. She could smell the grass and the trees, and a faint, haunting tang of lilac, and the breeze was soft against her skin.

"Edward?" Clare began on a self-conscious pretence of considering the question, and then recklessly abandoned it and cried: "Oh, Jenny, he's quite perfect! I can't begin to describe him—sort of fairish and not particularly tall, but he has the most lovely eyes—they can laugh at you without being in the least unkind. Do you know what I mean? And he's so understanding and so utterly reliable.

Oh dear—it doesn't make him sound a bit romantic, does it? But I do love him so terribly much. I can't help myself—I keep telling myself it's not suitable, it could never come to anything, but still it hurts most desperately when I'm not with him, and it's such heaven when I am!"

She was twisting and twisting a thin scarf between her hands so that Jenny feared for its survival. Jenny was vastly impressed and intrigued; she had never known Clare in quite such a state before. Their college life had been moderately flirtatious, but there had never been anything really serious. Sometimes they had talked it over together and had come to the conclusion that the average student was unimpressive; an older man was what they both wanted, but since none was readily available they preferred to wait. It was an admission of their own immaturity, perhaps.

"But why is it so unsuitable?" she demanded now. "Is he married, or something?"

"Oh, no. In a way it's worse. I mean, if he were married then I suppose I could at least hope that one day he'd be free again. But you see, Jenny —he's forty. And I'm only twenty. It's a big gap, isn't it? When I'm forty he'll be sixty. When I'm sixty he'll be eighty. It can't ever get any better."

"Dear me!" said Jenny. "Is that all?"

"But it's such a big all! Twenty years—as long as I've been alive. I'm certain that Mummy and Daddy wouldn't approve. Besides, I don't know that he's in the least interested in me. He's friendly and kind and helpful, and I can talk to him—but he's the same with everybody, not just me. He probably sees me as a little girl still."

"I'd have thought he must have noticed a certain difference."

They were coming up now through the kitchen gardens, past the old stable yard and under the shadow of the castle walls. Suddenly it was colder. Jenny became uncomfortably aware of the great height of solid stone above them, and of its vast weight and thickness pressing into the ground. She looked up, and saw white clouds dizzily floating beyond grey battlements in an infinite blue sky.

"Do you ever come this way at night?" she asked, and suddenly shivered.

"Oh, yes! It's beautiful in the moonlight—quite absurdly romantic. And the gardens smell heavenly."

Jenny wondered whether she would get so used to the size of the place that it would appear to her principally romantic by moonlight. Just now she found it sinister and oppressive.

They came round the sweep of gravel to the main entrance. A few people were standing by the balustrade of the broad terrace, gazing out over the precipitous gardens and the grey sea of trees beyond, but there was no crowd. Clare took Jenny in past a table where tickets were being sold—a large, capable-looking woman who nodded and smiled at them—and into the high, stone-vaulted entrance

21

hall. This opened in turn upon a vast, cathedral-like main hall, echoing and chill, with glassy marble floor and pillars, and lofty lancet windows along one side. It was splendid, but very gloomy, like a church.

"They never lived in it, did they?" asked Jenny, whispering in response to the cathedral atmosphere.

"Lord, no! It was all done to impress the neighbours. It's much nicer upstairs. I'll show you all that's open—come on."

The stairs branched up from a further chamber to one side of the hall. It was a double staircase of surprising delicacy, ornamented and balustraded by a wealth of stone tracery like frozen lace. They took the side which led almost directly into the Long Gallery, a sombre, Tudor-furnished place hung with portraits and paintings quite beyond price, the best of the famous Langton Collection. There was a Holbein, a Caravaggio, a Reynolds, Van Dyke and Rembrandt—Jenny had seen nothing to equal it outside the London galleries. She lingered, longing to stop and gaze her fill, but Clare urged her on.

"Just a quick tour today, and then the gardens. You'll have weeks to explore properly. But I do so want you to meet Edward."

The rooms seemed to unroll one from the other like a filmed journey. She had encountered so much that was new today; her head began to reel with the magnificence of it all, the gilding and carving and panelling, the plasterwork and the pictures and the elegant, uncomfortable furniture. There were weapons and armour and military relics, rooms of Chinoiserie, stuffed birds and eggs and tiger skins, gold and silver plate and priceless china—too much to take in all at once. Every room seemed hung with pictures upon wall-coverings of old and faded silk; there were countless ragged, historic four-poster beds and lacquered fire-screens and cabinets. She could not digest them all—nor could she have found her way out of the maze of public rooms without Clare to guide her.

They came at last to the Print Room. It was a sort of backwater, a quiet, almost plain room set at one corner of the castle a little apart from the main flow of traffic. Glass cabinet tables took up most of the space, with green curtains laid across the glass to shield the precious contents from too much light. One wall was hung with pictures, the rest were covered with shelves full of old leather-bound books, and there was the faintly musty smell that goes with ancient bindings, ink and paper.

A man rose from a window seat as they came in. His eyes went first to Clare, and then to Jenny, and he smiled. At once it was apparent to Jenny why Clare had fallen in love with Edward Channing. There was nothing very remarkable about him except for that smile, but when he smiled it was as if the world grew warmer, as if one noticed for the first time how very good it was to be alive.

"Jenny, this is Edward Channing, who runs the whole place," Clare was saying in a noticeably breathless voice. "Edward, this is Jenny Rowland."

He took Jenny's hand, and his touch was firm and pleasant.

"How very nice of you to come and help us out," he said. "It was such a relief to all of us when Clare thought of you. I'm not sure how we would have managed otherwise."

"I'm rather glad she thought of me too." It was odd; one spoke the most ordinary words to him, and somehow he made them seem clever and amusing.

"We're doing a quick tour," said Clare. "I want Jenny to see the gardens, the daffodils and everything."

"Certainly she must see the daffodils, every one. But, Clare, if you have just a moment—there are some prints his Lordship wants sorted out for him to send back to London, and I'm not at all sure which ones he means. He says you know. Could you have a quick look? It ought not to take long—"

"But yes—oh of course I will." Clare was all at once pink and flustered, clearly longing to stay with Edward and yet unable to think what she could do about Jenny. It was only fair to oblige.

"If you like to steer me out of the house I could explore the gardens quite happily on my own," Jenny volunteered.

"Oh, but Jenny—"

"No, honestly, I don't mind. I shall be perfectly happy. I can always find my way back to the terrace, can't I?"

"But I feel I'll be neglecting you."

"Of course you won't." She smiled at Edward

Channing, who was listening to the exchange and watching them with a smile of amusement. "I shall enjoy walking in the gardens and pretending that they belong to me. But if you were there I'd never be able to convince myself."

"Well, if you're sure you don't mind—oh, Jenny, you are a dear!"

Clare was too transparently grateful. If Edward Channing did not understand the cause of so much gratitude he must be a rather stupid man—and Jenny did not for a moment think him stupid. But then, she found his own excuse for keeping Clare with him somewhat thin. Plausible enough on the face of it, but not able to stand up to a closer scrutiny.

She let Clare show her the way through the house and onto the terrace.

"There are steps down," Clare explained. "I mean, the whole thing goes down in levels, and you can't even get lost in the woods at the bottom because all the paths lead back into the garden. Don't worry about the time. I'll wait for you if I'm out first."

"Don't hurry, you mean." Jenny grinned at her. "He is nice, isn't he? I quite see what makes him so special. Do you really think the Earl wants those prints in such a great hurry?"

"Oh, Jenny—of *course* he does!"

"And Edward really couldn't have found them for himself?"

"You're just trying to get me into a state!" But Clare returned to the print room with very bright eyes and a heightened colour, and Jenny thought with satisfaction that Edward Channing would have to be a blind man not to be affected by such glowing beauty.

She found the steps from the terrace and began to make her way down through the gardens. There were winding little paths around the lawns and shrubs, with rose arches and pergolas above them. Every now and again she came upon some feature such as a seat, a statue or a fountain perfectly set against a backcloth of azalea or rhododendron, or perched on the edge of some precipitous drop. The views were breathtaking. It almost appeared that the trees had been sculpted so as to give glimpses and vistas of the vale and the spreading plain beyond, contrasting them with little quiet arbours and spinneys, here a delicate white Greek temple and there a rustic summer house of wood. Stone benches provided resting places where one might sit and gaze, breathing air laden with resinous pine or with the scent of grass and flowering shrubs. There was a great deal of fragrant jasmine, and the ground in places was a carpet of sweet-smelling primroses and tiny lilies. Under the trees and across the lawns great swathes of daffodils nodded, as though the wind had blown drifts of them, wild and inexpressibly beautiful.

At almost the foot of the hill, where the gardens were swallowed up in woods, Jenny sat on a stone bench and looked around her. The silence was immense. Birds called among the trees, but once her footfall had ceased there seemed to be no other sound. Restless, small breezes carried to her nostrils all the sweet, unfamiliar scents of the garden. Sun slanted golden over the treetops, falling with a faint lingering warmth on her skin. For a few moments she closed her eyes and simply listened to the silence.

It seemed the first time she had been really alone all that day. She could have done with just a little less excitement; she could have managed perhaps without Edward Channing. But that was ungenerous of her; she could not expect to have Clare all to herself, it wasn't in the nature of things. In any friendship between two girls there was an unwritten law giving precedence at all times to affairs of the heart, and she had no right to resent it now simply because her own heart remained so obstinately free. There had been no one in her life like Edward Channing. From time to time her mother had hopefully brought home young schoolmasters and the like, laying them at her feet rather in the manner of a clever retriever. Pleasant enough young men they had all been, but not one of them in the least degree special. Sometimes Jenny had wondered if she might be expecting too much of life, demanding that it should present her with a man so much above all the rest. Perhaps her dreams, her expectations were set too high. Looking around her she saw on every side marriages that one couldn't imagine had ever risen above the routine and humdrum. They were sensible alliances between sensible people without a spark of romance in them. But she didn't want marriage, if that was all it meant. She wanted to feel as Clare did about Edward; she wanted to be dazzled and confused and even hurt, knocked off her feet by love. Oh, she was willing enough. All that she lacked was opportunity, the necessary encounter with a man powerful enough to bowl her over.

There was John Morley, of course. But he was Clare's brother, and somehow that made him almost a brother of her own. Besides, he was too nice. There wasn't any spark between them; she could imagine that he would make a pleasant and reliable companion through life, but for her that would be all, and no amount of argument could make the feeling resemble anything like romantic love.

All around her the birds sang with a soft, liquid melancholy. She felt the first shadows of the trees touch her, chilling her skin until she shivered. Opening her eyes she looked about her at the perfect garden, and wanted all at once to weep for her own loneliness, for the yawning lack of purpose in her life.

She was no longer quite alone. At the edge of the wood, so deep in shadow that she might easily not have seen him, a man stood and watched her. As if realising that she had seen him he came forward, but hesitantly, with a suggestion of reluctance in his step. Perhaps he, too, would have preferred solitude. But she could not pretend that she had not seen him, and so she smiled as he came nearer.

"I thought everyone would have gone by now," he said. His voice was that of an educated, cultured man, quiet, and with just the faintest trace of a lisp in it. He was only moderately tall, but moved with a contained and easy grace, perfectly at home in those surroundings. Because the sun was behind him Jenny could not see much of his face, only that the eyes were grey and the features regular and well marked. Sunlight struck gleams of silver from the thick fair hair about his head.

He came towards her along the gravel path, and she watched him, bemused by the way he had sprung from nowhere like a character in a dream.

"Perhaps everyone else has gone," she said. "I don't know. I belong here."

"Do you really?" He came to a halt close by her, and stared. The grey eyes examined her from top to toe with a remarkable thoroughness. "Tell me more," he demanded, and sat down on the other end of the stone bench.

Her impulse to say that she belonged had been foolish. But she had felt an irresistible urge to lay claim, to boast a little, to make the point that she was no mere visitor who had paid to come here.

"Oh," she said now, defensive, "I work here, that's all. Not quite the same as belonging, perhaps."

"That's interesting. Where do you work, exactly?"

"In the house. The Print Room." She began a little to resent his curiosity. It was no business of his, after all, and the more she had to explain it, the more illusory became her sense of really belonging.

"The gardens are beautiful, aren't they?" she said, changing the subject.

"Ah, but you should see them in summer. They were designed to be at their best then, I think."

"You've been here before, then?" she asked him.

"Quite often. I find it restful."

The sun had slipped behind the trees, leaving a strange clarity of light in the valley where they sat. Jenny found she could see the stranger's face in detail now. There was a pronounced Englishness about him, a boyishness in the clean-cut features, and yet they had strength and sensitivity, and there was a shrewdness about the way he looked at her, so that she found herself thinking how uncomfortable it would be to have to deceive such a man.

"What's your name?" he asked her now, unexpectedly.

"Jenny," she told him. "Jenny Rowland." For some reason she became suddenly aware of the beating of her own heart, and felt that even he must hear it, it was so loud. "What's your name?" she demanded, feeling a need to defend herself somehow.

"Charles," he told her.

"Charles what?"

"Oh—" He shrugged, looking amused. "Charles will do. It's what my friends call me. Tell me, then, what you think of Langton Castle. I'd like to hear the inside story—coming, I mean, from someone who actually works there. You must get to know quite a bit, one way or the other."

Three

He was a journalist, then. The muck-raking kind, presentable enough to mix with the kind of society he pilloried, but devoid of the least pity for them. Jenny felt obscurely let down. She had thought him rather an impressive kind of person until now, with his easy, confident manner and the grey eyes that seemed to see so much. But if he were hoping for a spicy story from her, then he was going to be disappointed.

"Really, there's nothing to tell," she said. "You can pay the entrance fee and see the house for yourself. I'm sure the Earl would rather you did. Then he'd at least make a little money on the deal."

"You think he makes much on this business of opening the house to all and sundry?"

"I suppose he must. Why else do it?"

"Oh, I don't know. The fellow might have a social conscience. D'you think he has?"

"You mean, do I think he feels bound to share his castle with the rest of the world?" She felt muddled by her own conflicting responses. On the one hand she experienced a deep dislike of being asked such questions by this man, who only wanted to get some kind of a story out of her that could be worked into something detrimental to the Langtons. On the other hand she had no real sympathy for anyone so rich as the Earl.

"I suppose, if his conscience were all that active, he could let in the public for nothing," she said at last. "But he doesn't. So he must make something out of it." She could imagine the headline: LANGTON EMPLOYEE SAYS EARL IN BUSINESS ONLY FOR THE MONEY.

"But I daresay there are overheads," her inquisitor pointed out. "Heating, cleaning, lighting, staff—that sort of thing."

"You sound as if you were on his side!" exclaimed Jenny.

"But you aren't?"

"How should I be?" She shrugged, irritated. "I'm only one of the *hoi polloi*, after all. It's the merest accident that I'm working here for a while. I don't exist in his world except as a paying customer—I live in a small suburban semi with a mother who works for her living, and that puts me socially quite beyond the pale, doesn't it?"

"Do they really keep you at arm's length? The family, I mean, these aristocratic Langtons?"

"Oh—" She laughed, a little shamefaced. "To tell the truth, I've never met them, so I couldn't tell you anything about them even if I wanted to. But it's fairly obvious, isn't it? I mean, they're rich and titled, and they mix with their own sort. However democratic society may have become, I still don't belong to their world. Look—" She gestured towards the garden, the lovely daffodil-starred green of the terraced lawns, and above them the castle still golden and glowing in the afternoon sun. It was heart-achingly beautiful. "It's all theirs," she said. "The public may come and look, provided they behave themselves and pay their money. But at closing time they have to go, and pay again next time. It doesn't belong to them. Maybe it seems unreasonable, but I do find it hard to approve of the one man who does own it all. What has he ever done to deserve it? He has so much, and there are people who have so very little, and nothing to choose between them so far as deserving goes. There are people, you know, who couldn't even afford to come and look."

He listened attentively and with a certain gravity, as if he were really concerned to know what she thought. When she had done he nodded, and looked again at the gardens and up at the castle, as if considering them in the light of her words.

"Of course," he said, "it's always possible that Langton himself would agree with every word you've said. He may think all that, and still be unable to find a solution. I mean, one can't give away a castle like a cake, in small pieces. It wouldn't be a castle any more, would it? Just a lot of meaningless stones."

"Oh, I don't pretend to know the answer," admitted Jenny. "I only know what I feel about it."

"I'm surprised that you should want to work here, feeling as strongly as all that."

"I didn't especially. But I was unemployed, you see, and the work's with pictures, and that's my speciality. Besides, I came to be with a friend who lives here."

"Ah. Then you must be part of their world, after all."

"She only lives on the estate," Jenny hastened to say. "Just another of the workers." She began to regret that she had said so much. One didn't say such things to perfect strangers—even though this one was so easy to talk to, and so perceptive. But then it was part of his trade to get people talking.

The shadows around them had grown deeper. On top of its hill the castle was a corona of fire blazing against the dark blue of the sky. Shivering suddenly, Jenny got stiffly to her feet.

"It's getting late. I have to go. I hadn't meant to spend so long in the garden."

He rose also, courteous and regretful.

"I'm sorry if I have detained you. But I was interested in what you had to say. I've enjoyed talking to you."

She felt absurdly shy, and found it difficult to meet his grey eyes, though now they smiled at her.

"I ought not to have been so outspoken," she said awkwardly. "Really I haven't anything against the Earl—I haven't even met the man. It's just what he stands for that I don't like."

"Perhaps when you do meet him you may find him quite a reasonable sort of fellow. Quite a few people do."

"I doubt if I shall meet him. I'd imagine he avoids

the castle when the visiting hordes are swarming over it."

"Oh, I rather think he likes to keep an eye on things. Make sure, you know, that none of his minions is fiddling the takings." He smiled, and held out a hand. "I'm so glad we met."

His smile, she thought suddenly, was very like Edward Channing's. It had the same power to bathe one in warmth and liking. She put her hand into his and wished that she had not to go, that she could stay and discover more about him. They had talked without her learning much about him, whereas he had gained a great deal of information about her. It had been cleverly done. Impulsively, she decided to add to his store of knowledge.

"I do hope we shall meet again," she said. "I'm staying for the summer with the Morleys. Leonard Morley, you know, trains the Earl's horses." There. It was done. If he wanted to find her he could; there was nothing else she could do to encourage him.

"I'm sure we shall meet again." His fingers seemed to tighten fractionally over hers before he let her hand go. His eyes, grey and steady, rested on her as if they approved of what they saw. She suddenly found it unaccountably difficult to breathe.

"Goodbye, then." She turned away.

" *Au revoir*," he said deliberately.

She knew that he was watching her as she began to climb the steep path from the bottom of the garden. Her knees felt stiff, and she found it hard to walk naturally, not to break into a run. It seemed a long and tortuous climb to the level grass terrace above the shadowed dell. When she had reached more level ground she dared to turn and look back, and found that he was still watching. He raised a hand then before turning away to the path by which he had come out of the wood. In a moment she could see him no longer; the deep shadow of the trees swallowed him.

Where could he be going? she wondered. Perhaps there was a short cut to the car park. A strange man, appearing and disappearing like that—a disturbing man; it was absurd, but her whole body felt shaken by her encounter with him, and weak, as if she had been running hard. The trouble was, she had lived quietly in her suburb for too long; she wasn't at all used to talking with attractive, intelligent men, and lack of practice put her at a decided disadvantage.

Clare was waiting on the upper terrace when at last Jenny reached it. Such was her state of exaltation that she quite failed to notice anything odd in Jenny's manner.

"Have you enjoyed the gardens? And, oh, Jenny, do tell me—do you really think Edward just wanted my company? Isn't he quite perfect? Really, there was nothing very much to sorting out the pictures the Earl wanted, it took only a minute or two, but he seemed to want to talk—only I don't dare to let myself hope. Do you think I'm being foolish? Jenny, please tell me—don't be afraid to tell the truth."

It was hard for Jenny to switch off her own preoccupation with the encounter just past. But Clare was in no state to listen to an account of it, and besides, it was hardly worth telling—everything that mattered had gone on in her own head. So she focused her thoughts on Edward Channing, and was able to report that she found him entirely satisfactory.

"Of course he wanted you to himself, you goose! Anyone with half a good eye could have seen it. I told you, I like him, and I don't think you at all foolish."

"But—you don't think him too old?"

"Old? Rubbish! He's one of those people who never seem any particular age. It's irrelevant, it doesn't count—he has so much charm one doesn't notice anything else."

And he was not in the least dangerous. That was where he most differed from the stranger she had encountered in the garden. Charles whoever-he-was had just the same kind of charm as Edward Channing, but there was an element of danger in it—too much intelligence, perhaps, too sharp a perceptiveness for comfort. Perhaps that was why he had disturbed her so.

"I'm being selfish," discovered Clare, becoming contrite. "But you understand, don't you, Jenny? And you'll forgive me? Being in love does make one quite appallingly selfish, that's one of the main things I've learned about it. Tell me what you thought of the gardens. Did you really enjoy your walk?"

"The gardens are absolutely beautiful, and I did enjoy it. Everywhere smelt of spring." But she could not bring herself to mention her encounter with the stranger. It was private, somehow, like a special dream, to be remembered and gone over in her head but not to be shared. "I'm hungry," she said instead. "It must be the country air. Did you say we were expected back for tea?"

They returned to Clare's home on the further slope of the hill, wandering peacefully across the rough grassy parkland, pausing every now and again to look back at the castle growing dim against the darkening sky. Clouds were spreading in from the horizon.

"A dull day tomorrow," commented Clare. "But it won't actually rain. I know. I can feel these things in my bones."

A light or two had gone on in the castle.

"Who lives in it when the family's away?" Jenny wanted to know. "Do they keep a full-time staff?"

"Only a few. Edward has a flat there, and the housekeeper and a maid or two, that's all. The gardeners live over the stables, and other estate people about the park or in the village."

"Do they bring all the rest with them from London, then?"

"There isn't any 'rest'—apart from a cook, I believe. When they're here they have a woman in sometimes, and one of the gardeners doubles as butler for anything grand. All the other people who work here are simply maintenance staff, and there's a small army of them."

"I suppose there must be." Overheads, thought Jenny, remembering her conversation with the stranger in the garden. Somebody had to pay them. Perhaps it was fair, after all, that the public should contribute. She looked back, and wondered from whose rooms the lights shone. Impossible to believe that she would ever learn to find her way about the monstrous great place or learn to identify from outside the many rooms within.

There was a high tea waiting for them when they got back to Morleys. Clare's mother was apologetic.

"Quite often we have to do things this way rather than dining properly, because of the odd times Leonard and John work. There's a mare about to foal, and they can't leave her, she may have trouble, poor thing. So one couldn't sit down to a hearty dinner in the circumstances. But you can all the sooner go off and gossip to your heart's content, and then fill up later with buns and cocoa if you want to. I shall feed the men whenever they get in."

Heroically Jenny quelled the temptation to confess that she hardly ever 'dined'. It might have sounded sour, and she had no wish to be ungrateful. This was the way Clare's family thought it normal to live; it probably had never occurred to them that there was any other way. One couldn't resent it, they were much too charming. In the end she and Clare took a pot of cocoa up with them and sat in Jenny's room by the glow from the electric fire and gazed out of the window at the castle's lighted windows.

From this distance they might have been any windows. There was no hint of the great hulk of stone all around them; night had eaten it away.

"I *think* that one's the Earl's library," said Clare doubtfully. "I'm not just sure of how the private rooms go. Edward took me round them once when the family was in London, and of course we've been to meals there, but I don't clearly remember."

"You get invited to dinner, do you?"

"Well—lunch or tea, usually. Dinner tends to be reserved for their particular friends. Mummy and Daddy go sometimes. And John. Jenny—do you like John?"

"Why, yes—very much, what I've seen of him. Why?"

"Oh, well—I was wondering if I ought to tell you something, that's all."

"Clare—don't tell me! Let me guess. I have it—he's really not your brother at all, but only a step, and you were betrothed to him as a babe in arms and now the time has come to marry, and that's why you're afraid your parents won't let you marry Edward Channing. How's that?"

"Idiot!" Clare giggled. "It's nothing like that! But I feel I ought to tell you, because—well, just in case. Only you must promise to be close as the grave about it."

"As the grave!" Jenny declared, and waited.

"Well," began Clare, and her voice had taken on a note of real solemnity, as if what she had to tell genuinely impressed her; "you know the Earl has a younger sister? Her name's Rowena, and she and my brother John are terribly in love. Only they can't do anything about it because of who she is. Her mother would never let her marry something so lowly as the family horse-doctor."

"Is that what he is?" said Jenny, momentarily

diverted. "But I'd have thought it quite an important thing to be, especially if he's a good one. Oh, really, Clare—you can't be serious? Such a Victorian way of looking at things! Why doesn't he simply run away with her?"

"Mostly because of Daddy. Think of the effect it would have on him, the impossible situation it would make between him and the family. He and the Earl get on so well, they've built up such a string of horses. Besides, what would it do to John's own career? One simply can't make that sort of grand romantic gesture. In books maybe, but not in real life."

Real life, Jenny thought, being so much tied up with money and class. But she said, "I suppose not. Pity. So what do they plan to do about it?"

"I don't know. Wait and see, I should think. It's about all they can do, really."

"Perhaps the Family will unbend."

"Perhaps. Unless in the meantime Rowena lets herself be talked into marrying for the sake of a financial alliance or something ghastly. They still do, you know; this family marries into that so as to combine their shares and take over a company or redistribute property or carry on a name. I've known it happen. Barbarous, really."

"Mediaeval," Jenny agreed sombrely. It would have been unbelievable, but for the fact that she had seen Langton for herself and begun to understand something of the burdens wealth and rank might place upon people who believed that they mattered still. "Edward said something about the family coming here on their way to Tathwell, didn't he?" she asked after a moment.

"Yes—tomorrow, I think. Unless that light is in the Earl's library and means that he's already arrived. Sometimes he comes ahead of the others to get a bit of work done before they arrive. The Dowager tends to expect him to socialise, so the poor man's a bit hard pressed when she's here."

"I'd like to see them." She had found so much to say to the stranger in the garden about Lord Langton; it would be interesting to see what the man was actually like.

"Oh, you'll be bound to see them. Well, Langton and Rowena, anyway. He's always about the place, and she—well, you can imagine. The horses are an amazing magnet. And if Lola has her foal all right—"

"Clare, do you know," said Jenny, "I have this curious feeling that I've stepped into a picture book. Nothing seems quite real any more. The world is full of fairy-tale castles and gardens and star-crossed lovers, earls and countesses and beautiful horses. I've got mental indigestion."

"You must be worn out!" Clare was at once contrite. "You've had such a day, the journey here and all the new places and people, and now I sit rabbiting on about my family and the Langtons. I ought to be shot."

"Oh, I wasn't complaining. Though now you come to mention it, I am tired."

"Then it's a hot bath and bed for you. I insist. After all, you start work tomorrow, and I'm responsible for getting you there fighting fit."

Jenny allowed herself to be bullied. It was a comforting sensation to be organised by someone; it made her feel less alien, less of an outsider. She soaked gratefully in the luxurious half-sunken bath, and tried to imagine what it must feel like to take all this for granted, a bathroom with thick cream carpet, mirror walls and a separate shower cabinet—and not even the family bathroom, but Clare's own.

I shall find it hard to go back to being me, she thought. I'd like to be able to stay, never to have to leave here. I belong—I was right after all when I told the man in the garden that. I do belong, because it's the way I've always wanted to live. It's me.

But she could not approve of her own feelings. Here she lay, wallowing in scented luxury, and she had done nothing to deserve it. In a small way she was guilty of exactly what she blamed the Langtons for; she was living off privilege, and enjoying it and wanting more. All the same, how could she have refused? It was just the way things had turned out—doubtless Lord Langton felt much the same about his lands and titles. The fighting for them had all been done long ago, and not by him; was there any harm in his enjoying what had come to him by chance?

It was a confusing problem, and her mind was too foggy to grapple with it now. She climbed out of the bath and enveloped herself in a huge, shaggy bath towel. Reflected in the mirror walls she looked like a Womble, not at all a romantic figure, and not in the least tormented by conscience. She wondered where the man from the garden was at this moment. Perhaps it was as well he could not see her; he might have found it hard to take her ideas seriously just now.

Clare had turned down the bed and closed the curtains at the dormer window. The room glowed with light from a cream-shaded bedside lamp, inviting and warm and already home. Jenny's travelling clock ticked on the bedside table.

"I'll call you in the morning, if you like," Clare suggested. "Breakfast will wait till we're ready. We don't have to be at the castle until after lunch—the visitors actually come in at one thirty. But I suppose just tomorrow we ought to go up in the morning so that you can get the hang of things."

"Whatever you say. I'm longing to browse in that Print Room. And then, of course, for you there's the magnet of Edward."

"Idiot!" But Clare blushed. "Come to that, you may get your first peep at the Earl. While you were in the bath I went down to ask after Lola's foal—which has arrived all right—and I heard then that he did come today."

"I can't wait to meet him." But the sarcasm sounded a little unconvincing even to Jenny. "And the rest of his tribe?" she asked.

"Due tomorrow evening. John's trying very hard to pretend that it doesn't concern him, and anyone with half an eye could see that he's lit up like a Christmas tree. I can't imagine how they think they can go on keeping it dark, he and Rowena."

"I don't know. People can be amazingly blind to

something they don't expect to see, can't they?" Sitting up in bed, Jenny wrestled with a vexatious problem of her own. She was not sure that pride allowed her to confess ignorance in the matter— but then there was no reason why she should be expected to know anything so obscure, and anyway Clare would understand.

"Clare," she ventured, feeling uncommonly foolish, "I know that an Earl is Lord So-and-so when you refer to him in the third person. But if the occasion were to arise—which I know it probably won't—and I had to speak to Lord Langton, what would I call him? I don't suppose 'hey, Earl' would be quite the thing, would it?"

"You should hear some of the American tourists! Honestly, Jenny, he probably wouldn't mind—he's not a bit stuffy, I promise you. But if you want to be correct, and as you don't know him yet, you simply call him Lord Langton. Most people seem to call him just by his Christian name."

"And what's that?" asked Jenny.

"Charles," said Clare. "Charles Nicholas Aubrey Derringer, Earl of Langton, if you want the lot—but he prefers just Charles. He says the rest makes him feel nervous."

Four

Jenny lay in bed in the darkness feeling as though a tub of cold water had been thrown over her.

She had not dared to tell Clare. She hadn't even needed to ask what Charles Langton looked like; she already knew. There could be no question of coincidence.

Over and over again in her mind she went through their conversation. There was the way he had avoided giving a surname, the way he had been so surprised to find her there after he thought everyone had gone, his close questioning when she claimed to belong there—even his defence of the Earl when she had been at such pains to attack him. Had she not been so full of her own ideas and importance she must have realised who he was. But she had been utterly self-absorbed. Without pausing to consider their effect she had aired her wretched views, opinionated and insufferably smug as they were—and all the time he must have been seething inside. Or, more probably, laughing at her, which was infinitely worse.

What on earth was she to do now? According to

Clare, it would be quite impossible to get through the summer without at some point running into him. In any case he was bound to mention the episode to someone, Edward Channing, perhaps, or Leonard Morley—conceivably he might even object to her presence on the estate, since she had made so clear to him her disapproval of the whole operation.

Miserably she cast about in her mind for some means of escape, some way she could miraculously put things right. But there was none. She was forced to face the probability that she had ended her visit almost before it was begun, by insulting the Earl of Langton at first meeting. She might as well pack her bags now.

All the same, it had been unfair of him to let her go on so. He ought to have told her who he was. If the home truths he had heard had annoyed him, no one was to blame more than himself. Assurance of this gave her a little courage; the fault hadn't been quite all on her side, and her impression of him, even now that she knew his identity, was of a reasonable man. Surely he wouldn't condemn her for speaking her mind? She had tried to be honest; she could not remember having said anything that might be construed as a betrayal of confidence—indeed, she had made it quite plain that there were no confidences for her to betray. She knew as yet almost nothing about the Langtons.

Back and forth in her head the arguments went, at one moment hopeful, at the next black with despair, until she had worried herself at last into an uneasy sleep. But all through her sleeping there were moments not quite of dream nor yet of waking, when she seemed once more to see him standing between her and the sun, his hair like silver, his face in shadow. And always she could see his eyes, cold and grey, and they seemed to look into her and through her as though she had no more substance than a drift of mist.

Morning came at last, heavy and dark with cloud. When Clare came to wake her with a cup of tea, Jenny had already made up her mind what she must do.

"About Lord Langton," she said. "Tell me—is he fair and medium built and quite youngish, with just the faintest hint of a lisp when he speaks?"

"Why, yes. How did you know? He's terribly attractive, especially that trace of a lisp—reminds one of Humphrey Bogart," Clare mused. "A vulnerable spot in a strong man."

"I met him yesterday," confessed Jenny. Clare plumped herself down on the end of the bed, astonished.

"You never told me!"

"I didn't know who he was. I imagined he must be a visitor. Clare—he asked me what I thought about the castle and the family and so on, and—well, I'm afraid I came out with some pretty strong stuff. Left wing, you know—fair shares for all, down with the aristos, that sort of thing."

Clare gurgled with laughter and hugged herself delightedly.

"Serve him right!" she crowed. "He will go about anonymously mingling! Oh, Jenny—you haven't been worrying about it all night, have you? Honestly, he isn't the kind to make an issue of it. In fact he probably agreed with every word you said, only he's not in a position to do very much about it, is he?"

"Do you really think so? I mean, do you think he'll consider me responsible enough to stay and work in the Print Room? But, Clare, I practically told him his way of life was immoral!"

"And so it is. But it's the way things are, and we can't change them, not all at once. He does his best, you know. Of course he'll let you stay—he probably admired you no end for speaking out for what you believe in. But, Jenny—you don't think *us* immoral, do you? I mean, I know we're well off, but Daddy and Mummy and John do *work*—"

"Oh, of course I don't mean you! I mean the Langtons, people with vast inherited wealth, castles and country houses. I mean them," said Jenny miserably, hating herself for a Puritan and a killjoy.

"I hadn't realised you felt so strongly that way," said Clare.

"Well I do. Only—I find it hard to dislike him personally. Langton, I mean. In fact I rather liked him. It's just what he stands for that I can't get over."

"Then you're going to have to subdue your conscience, aren't you?" Clare said cheerfully. "Now that you know him, be nice to him. You might even end up a countess."

"Pigs might fly!" But Jenny felt much better. She still did not relish the prospect of her inevitable meeting with Lord Langton, but at least she no longer saw ruin staring her in the face.

She dressed carefully in a sober, plain oatmeal woollen suit with gold chain at the neck. Her face, as she examined it in the mirror, was pale; the uneasiness of the night showed in a smudginess about the eyes and in the almost translucent whiteness of her skin. It wasn't a bad face, all the same, having the sort of bones that outlast girlish prettiness. A good work-a-day face, she thought, with a certain steadiness about it—not a fool's face. Even Charles Langton couldn't have taken it for that, however much of a fool she might have made of herself just the once.

The girls breakfasted alone; everyone else had got up earlier and gone about the day's business already. They walked up the hill to the castle under a grey sky, though the air was soft and not really cold. There was no wind to set the daffodils nodding.

"I'll show you the catalogue of what's in the Print Room," said Clare as they walked. "People ask to see specific things sometimes, so you need to know what's on the shelves as well as what's on display. You'll have to mug up the history bit too—there's a typed account somewhere, I'll find it for you. And I expect you'd like a better look at the paintings in the gallery."

"I would. There are some marvellous things."

"And the most horrific security system. It's the nightmare of my life that one day I'll forget myself and take down one of the watercolours and set the whole alarm system clanging. It's the most appalling noise."

"But necessary, I suppose."

"Well—there are pictures one couldn't begin to put a price to."

All wrong, Jenny thought despite herself. So much wealth in the hands of one family. But at least they did let people come and look, for a price.

The castle today looked dark and forbidding, its walls massive, its pinnacles and battlements grey as the sky beyond. Inside, there were lights switched on, and all along the vaulted corridors women were busy with mops, polishers and dusters. Jenny followed Clare up the branching stairs and through the warren of echoing apartments to the Print Room. It was strange, seeing the house like this, very much a theatre before curtain-rise; an odd, prosaic feeling, as if all the glamour and the magnificence were held in abeyance until the show should begin. One couldn't imagine that anyone, at any time in its history, had ever thought of the place as home.

In contrast, the Print Room was quiet and cosy. Clare switched on the strip lights above the display cabinets, and looked round her with evident pleasure.

"Snug!" she said. "Our esoteric little retreat from the noisy world. And to think that they pay us for spending our time here!"

"I keep forgetting that. I don't feel employed," said Jenny. "Oughtn't I to have signed something?—a contract, or an oath of fealty perhaps?"

"Edward will be round sometime with the papers," Clare reassured her. "You'll feel more business-like after the briefing. We all meet in the Long Gallery each day just before opening time—usually only hello and is everybody here, but sometimes little things crop up that we need to know about."

"Speech to the troops before battle? Well—you'd better start instructing me, hadn't you? I don't want to be caught napping by some eager bibliophile on my first day."

So Clare began to explain the room. An hour went by unnoticed, during which Jenny made herself familiar with the catalogue and contents of the room, and with the history of many of its treasures. There were engravings after Holbein, and drawings by Van Dyke and Turner and many others; there were the designs for the present castle and engraved plates of the old; there were water-colours and prints of all kinds, some immensely valuable and some of purely local interest. She found sketches and mezzotints made by a former countess, and furniture and carpet designs by Robert Adam. There were even scenery and costume drawings by a Langton younger son who had scandalised his family in the late nineteenth century by getting mixed up with the theatre.

Eventually her head became so stuffed with novelties that she could take in no more.

"I shall simply forget it all again," she said to Clare. "I need a change of scale. Is it all right if I go and ogle the pictures in the Long Gallery?"

"You go and ogle. I'll tidy up here and wait a little just in case—well, in case anyone comes."

"You think he will?" Jenny teased her. "I'm sure

he would, if only he knew you were here. But does he?"

The cleaners had finished with the Long Gallery. It stood silent, the strip of dull crimson carpet clean and empty, gilded chairs and console tables neatly fenced off by swags of scarlet rope. Jenny would have liked more light by which to examine the pictures, but she dared not switch them on. Enough dull illumination seeped in at the high windows to make the bigger canvases visible, though their colours were subdued—but then, the painters had made them in light much like this, not by the artificial glare of neon strips.

It was a collection to set the senses reeling. Each generation of Langtons seemed to have possessed unerring discrimination; they had been painted by the best talent that money could buy, and they had spared nothing to acquire pictures by the most exalted masters. At one end of the gallery hung a vast Caravaggio, and at the other a set of four exquisite small Breughels. Along the great panelled wall between were the family portraits by Gainsborough, Kneller, Lely, Lawrence, Reynolds, Zoffany—it was like a history of English painting all collected beneath one roof.

She came to a halt before a full length portrait of the tenth Earl, painted by Hoppner. Leaning negligently against the bole of a tree, he wore hunting costume, a loose top coat and knee breeches, and a shirt carelessly open at the neck. Wind tugged the fair hair into a fine dishevelment above a face whose features might have been exactly those she had struggled to recall throughout the night. It was an intelligent, wilful, humorous face, and had she only looked more closely at the portrait yesterday she would have been in no doubt as to the identity of the stranger in the garden. The tenth and the fifteenth Earl might have been twin brothers, the resemblance was so strong.

"Good morning, Jenny."

His voice spoke very close to her shoulder. He must have come quietly along the carpet, and she had not heard him; she gave a wild start of alarm, and whirled round to confront him, her face hot and her mouth gone dry. He was regarding her with a faint smile, amused, at ease, without the least trace of embarrassment or constraint. Just for a moment she felt a small flare of resentment, but it was quickly lost in confusion as she remembered again some of the things she had said to him at their last meeting.

"Oh, good morning," she said helplessly. "You startled me—I didn't hear you."

"Do you admire my Hoppner? They say it resembles me—I often wonder if we think alike too, the tenth Earl and I. But I rather doubt it."

Jenny turned back for a moment to the portrait. Its hard grey eyes stared challengingly down at her. A wild man, she thought, who took what he wanted without much care for others. Magnificent to look at, but not a nice person to know.

"I hope you don't think like him," she said. "I'm not at all sure that I'd care for his thoughts."

"I'm so glad. He was one of the blackest sheep of

54

the family." He smiled at her now with genuine liking, as if she had said the right thing, as if he had made up his mind about her. His charm seemed to reach out and touch her with physical warmth, disturbing her, dazzling her eyes so that she found it hard to look at him. She did not know what to say. There had never been anyone before who had made her feel so shy, so much at a loss.

"You see, I do work here," she said at last. "Yesterday you didn't believe me."

"I couldn't be sure. I hadn't heard about the arrangement, you see—and I do normally like to know everyone who works in or around the castle. Perhaps you can forgive me, in the circumstances."

"If you can forgive the things I said. I'm afraid I was horribly opinionated and rather objectionable."

"Indeed you weren't." He seemed concerned that she should take this view of the matter. "You said what you thought quite reasonably and with every right to do so. I prefer to hear the truth from people."

"But I was so dogmatic! Nothing's that black and white. You can't help the fact that you inherited this castle—and I'm sure you do your best with it."

"Oh, I do." He was laughing at her now, just a little. "But you mustn't be influenced in your thinking by the fact that you may find the rich and powerful also quite likeable. Of course they are—they have no reason not to be, life is good to them. Don't let yourself be too easily disarmed."

"Now you're arguing against yourself!"

"I frequently do." Still smiling, he put a hand under her arm and steered her towards one of the deep window recesses where there were seats. "Come and tell me about yourself. I like to know all about the people who work for me—it helps me to feel that I own the place."

She sat facing him, folding her hands in her lap, feeling absurdly shy and inadequate. She was very much aware of the grey eyes that steadily surveyed her, and of his nearness, which disturbed her in a way that she had never experienced before.

"There's not much to tell about me," she said. "I'm a friend of Clare's, we were at college together, and both got a Fine Arts diploma at the same time. I live with my mother, who's a teacher, and I was out of work. That's all, really."

"A relatively blameless existence, so far." He was teasing her still. "Convenient for us, though. I hope you'll enjoy the summer here, even if you do disapprove of us."

"Oh, please—"

"Very well. We'll forget about that—for the moment. I do wish you well in the job. It's an aspect of the business very much after my own heart; I could give up the castle and title without a pang, but not the pictures or the books."

"Do you feel as if they actually belong to you?" She was not quite sure how to put it. "I mean—they seem so vast, so impersonal. I can't imagine ever being able to feel that a Caravaggio belonged to me."

"There's a sense in which no picture can ever belong to anyone. But these are mine, make no mistake about it." For a moment then he looked very like the Hoppner portrait on the wall beyond him. "If it were not for my family, most of them would never have been painted. The people in them are my ancestors, I have grown up knowing them, and they are part of my inheritance."

"I hadn't looked at it like that." She tried to imagine what it must feel like, to know these painted people as individuals, as members of one's own family, the builders of one's own tradition. It must make for tremendous feelings of continuity with the past.

"You seem very determined to understand," he remarked.

"Of course. It interests me. I'd like to be able to understand it all—the business of heredity, I mean, family and class."

"Oh, that—" He shrugged and smiled, but with a kind of bitterness. "It's a classic operation of the closed shop, isn't it? Membership strictly limited to those who can afford to go to the right schools, keep the requisite number of horses, servants and so forth?"

"No," she found herself saying, somewhat to her own surprise. "It's more than that. It involves blood—it's to do with those people there." She gestured at the pictures on the walls of the gallery. "But I'm not sure that it can be explained. Not in words, anyway."

He considered her, silent and thoughtful, as if he were seeing her anew and found her more complex than he had at first imagined.

"Now it's you who are arguing against yourself," he said, but without conviction, as if the subject had exhausted itself in his mind. "Tell me, then—are you pleased to be staying with the Morleys? Do you like it there?"

"Oh, I do. Clare was my closest college friend, and her family are the most charming people. I can't imagine anywhere I'd rather be."

He smiled then.

"Nice to be young." It wasn't meant in any derogatory sense, only with a certain indulgent amusement, but she felt stung.

"Anyone would think you at least a hundred, and embittered with it!" she declared.

"Oh, I'm at least a hundred, sometimes much more. Blue blood runs thin, you know, in the end." But he was teasing again. All the same, she thought that there was a certain bitter undercurrent to the words, as if he really were not happy. In a sense she could understand it. He must perceive quite clearly the contradictory nature of his situation, a survival from the past in a modern world which by and large resented him. It couldn't be entirely comfortable to be a wealthy Earl in the last quarter of the twentieth century. And this one, she suspected, was more vulnerable than most, and suffered from the conflict of pride and conscience within himself.

The understanding profoundly disturbed her. Later, trying to describe to Clare the effect of what he had said, she found that she could not put it into words. It sounded corny, superficial, designed to wring an easy tear. But it had all made a very deep impression on her. She felt in some way involved, caught up in a dialogue that went to and fro all the time in her head, whose ending very much mattered to her in a more personal way than she could easily explain.

Clare at least partly understood.

"One gets terrific feelings of loyalty," she said. "A sort of family pride, I suppose, even though they aren't exactly one's own family. They matter, don't they? One can't write them off just as a survival from the past. They have power still."

They had, and Charles Langton particularly so.

"Remember I haven't met the others yet," Jenny said.

"You will. There's the Daffodil Ball next week. You'll see them then."

"What exactly is this Daffodil Ball?"

"Oh, it's super!" promised Clare. "A really grand, old-fashioned ball like they used to have before the wars, with the whole of the estate invited. There's champagne and dancing till dawn, and a tremendous buffet, and everyone mixes in."

"Daffodil because of the season, I suppose?"

"And because it's not the Corn Ball. That comes at the end of the season."

"It would."

"Well, I think it's a jolly good idea. One party to get the season going, and the other to celebrate its conclusion. It's one of the Langton traditions."

"Otherwise known as keeping the workers happy," commented Jenny. But she only half meant it. Somehow she could not think of the Langtons in quite those terms any more. Whether she liked it or not, she was involved with them, and could not criticise without at least a little damaging herself.

Five

The week seemed to pass very quickly in one respect. Jenny became accustomed to the daily walk up to the castle, the tranquil atmosphere of the Print Room, the stares of visitors and their sometimes bizarre questions. Occasionally there were more knowledgeable people to whom she could show the prints and books that were really interesting and not merely on display because of their connection with the Langtons. She enjoyed this, and enjoyed also the opportunity to make herself familiar with the work of engravers who had been real artists, who had taken pains to produce pictures both beautiful and technically excellent. It was like an extension of college, really, she and Clare working together in an Aladdin's cave of exquisite things.

But in another way, oddly, the week dragged. Every day she hoped that Charles Langton might look in on them, or that they might encounter him on their way through the halls and corridors of the castle. But he remained elusive.

"He's probably catching up on the accounts," said

Clare when Jenny, carefully casual, mentioned the subject. "Or looking over the estate. He's no absentee landlord, you know—he likes to be in touch with all that's going on. Daddy says he's a fine practical farmer, and that's an enormous compliment, believe me."

Jenny believed it. But then she could imagine that Lord Langton would make himself master of any subject that interested him. He had a conscience; he cared about people, and especially those whom he saw as his particular responsiblity. It was an admirable trait, and she liked him for it.

But he did not come near the Print Room. Then, after all, why should he? She became angry at her own conceit, telling herself that she had no reason to suppose him in the least concerned for her now that he had satisfied himself as to her general respectability and competence. She wasn't even one of the estate workers, merely an import for the season. Beyond her function in the smooth running of things she had no further significance.

It depressed her. Stupid, but she wanted to know him better. She wanted to understand the cause of his dissatisfaction with himself, even perhaps to help him—though that was going too far into the realms of fantasy, it was patently absurd, and she had to check it. All the same she wished that something perhaps might bring them together again just once, so that she might have a chance to satisfy her nagging sense of something left unfinished.

The Daffodil Ball took place on a Sunday, beginning late so that there was time for preparations to be made after the castle closed at five. Clare insisted that Jenny should take part of the afternoon off.

"You've worked like a Trojan all week, and really I can manage the last couple of hours on my own. You can give me some time next week, then. You look as if you need a break—are you sure you're not sickening for something? I do want you to enjoy the ball."

"I'm feeling neglected," confessed Jenny, joking perilously near the truth. "The lovely Lord hasn't been to see us all week. Can he possibly have found strength to resist me?"

Clare giggled.

"He's probably been locked in a tower by the Dowager Countess, who's heard rumours of your beauty."

"Is she possessive with him too?"

"As a she-dragon. Frightfully keen on preserving the blueness of the blood. Her father was a Duke, which means that she married just a little beneath her, and she can't forgive or forget."

"Strewth!" Jenny tried to be amused, but dismally failed. Listlessly she obeyed Clare's instructions, and took herself out into the castle gardens with her sketch block and pencils, hoping that to sit for a while in the sunshine and fresh air might indeed prove a remedy for the vague malaise that beset her. It was clearly absurd to have become so emotionally involved with a man she had met only twice—and a man, moreover, so far removed from her station in life that he might as well have lived on the moon for all the contact there was likely to be between them. She was making herself miserable over a day-dream—and miserable, what was more, at a time when she ought to have been revelling in the marvellous life into which she had been plunged. She was surrounded by charming people, there was beauty everywhere she looked, she had the chance of riding, swimming, tennis every day if she were so inclined. Yet she felt thoroughly down. Clare was uncomfortably perceptive. Although Jenny loved the place and the people and their whole way of life, yet she still felt the need of something more—and that was out of reach.

She sat on a low wall to one side of the middle terrace, facing a particularly delicate stone urn which she had meant to sketch when she had time. It was a gem of its kind, perfectly shaped and garlanded with the most exquisite little flowers, and set in place by someone who had known just what effect it could create against a background of green lawns and the distant, darker mass of trees.

Light fell on the rounded stonework of the vase and threw the carving into bold relief. She worked quickly before it should change, wanting to get down just the right feeling of delicacy and balance, the rightness of the thing in its garden setting. All the detail of the drawing must be in the urn and its stone plinth, with only enough background to place it. Her concentration was intense, so much so that she was quite unaware of the occasional castle visitors wandering by on the gravel path, or of the man who stood for some minutes a little way behind her, absorbedly watching.

She put down her pencil for a moment when the sketch was almost done, and straightened her back and flexed her fingers, looking ruefully at the pencil smudges on them.

"I hadn't realised you could draw so well," said Charles Langton, behind her.

Startled, her heart gave one great leap and then seemed to crouch quite still inside her. She whirled round, scattering sketch block and pencils over the ground.

"Oh dear," he said ruefully, coming forward to pick them up and then keeping the block in his hands. "I'm sorry—it wasn't fair to sneak up on you like that. But I didn't want to distract you from your drawing."

"Oh, that's all right." She was covered in confusion, her cheeks hot, her heart turning queerly over and over. All her limbs became suffused with a nervous aching. She had waited and wanted him to come all week, and now that he was here she half wished him away, because his presence disturbed her so. But he stood on the terrace beside her and looked long and hard at the drawing, and then at her. The sun caught his fair hair and made it almost white, but left his face in shadows, so that the grey eyes seemed bleak.

"It's not finished," she said quickly, defensive about her work. "There's a little still to do."

"But not much."

"No."

"It's good, and I like it," he said, his eyes returning to the block in his hands. "Have you done any more while you've been here?"

"Bits. A window, and a corner of the building, and a view along the top terrace."

"May I see them some time?"

"Of course, whenever you like. They're at Morleys. Would you like me to bring them—?"

"Perhaps I might call there? I shall have to see Leonard Morley again before I go, in any case."

"Oh." Dismay clutched at her. "You're going away?"

"Only to Tathwell. It's our other house, and a quieter place than this in summer. My mother much prefers it."

"Yes. I believe Clare told me."

"It isn't very far," he said, as if he sensed her dismay and wanted to reassure her. "Only a matter of twenty miles or so. I can keep an eye on things quite well from there." He wasn't looking at her, but at the drawing, and his expression became abstracted as if his thoughts had moved on to something else. Then he seemed to come to himself, and handed her back the drawing block, smiling. "You're very talented. You ought to be working more at this and less in my dismal castle."

"But it isn't dismal! And I'm learning all the time—from things in the Print Room, I mean."

"I hope you'll make use of all of it. I must ask Edward to let you see the private collection—there's a Leonardo drawing you'd like, and I have quite a few Constable and Turner sketches and so on."

"I'd love to see them." She was torn between pleasure in the suggestion and disappointment that he should not have offered to show her them himself. But then, he was leaving; he was going on to Tathwell.

"I hope you'll be here tonight," she said impulsively. "At the Ball, I mean."

"Oh yes. It wouldn't do to miss the Daffodil Ball. No doubt I shall see you there. But now I must leave you to finish your drawing. I hope the light hasn't quite gone." He seemed for a moment to hesitate, as if there were more he wanted to say, but then he smiled, inclined his head in a nod of farewell and turned away. She watched him go, and was filled with an intense, almost panic-stricken longing to call him back; it was as if he were going away from her for ever, and she felt that she could not bear it. But she had no reason for stopping him.

He walked up the long garden terrace by terrace until the steep incline of the ground at last hid him from sight. Not once did he look back. It was as if he had quite dismissed her from his mind, although her whole consciousness was filled with him. When she finally turned back to her drawing she found that her hands were unsteady and would not obey her. There was no point in going on with it. She could finish it another time, but not now—not since he had come to wreck her peace of mind and invade and disturb her whole being.

She gathered up her pencils and drawing block and bag, and started on cotton-wool legs back to Morleys. There, in the quiet house, she shut herself in the bathroom and lay for a long time in a hot, scented bath, and tried to analyse her feelings.

She might have thought herself in love, if the whole notion were not so utterly ridiculous. One didn't meet a perfect stranger—a belted Earl at that—and fall instantly in love with him. It was a fiction out of paperback romances, not something that could happen in real life. Admittedly he was attractive; he had all the charm, the distinction and gloss of a product of the best English public schools, and then there was the title, which despite everything did impress her. He had spoken of blue blood as a bitter joke, but there was after all some validity in the notion of good breeding. It was true of his horses, and so it had a relevance to him; he was the carrier of centuries of pride and privilege. No doubt he had inherited bad things too. She could imagine that if he were angry those cold grey eyes might be very hard to face, the pleasant voice capable of stinging like a whip.

But he had no reason at present to be angry with her. She longed to please him, to be noticed and thought about, to be sometimes in his head as he was in hers. It wasn't any use, she knew that; however close he might come to the ideal she carried in her imagination, she could never hope for love from him. But just for a little while she wanted him to notice her. Later she could summon up her defences—later, when he had gone away to Tathwell. Then she could practise resistance. But not just yet.

Clare came home radiant because Edward Channing had spent the last hour of the afternoon with her in the Print Room.

"He's asked me for the first and last dance and as many in between as I can spare!" she confessed, spreadeagled on Jenny's bed as Jenny brushed her hair dry in front of the electric fire. "That's practically a declaration, isn't it? Oh, Jenny—I've never felt like this before, so happy and so frightened!"

"You goose! He's the nicest man possible." The more Jenny had seen of him during the week, the more he had risen in her estimation. He was a quiet, steady, humorous man, a grown-up, and if she had not been so much dazzled by Charles Langton she might very well have fallen a little in love with him herself. "He's right for you," she said. "I'm utterly convinced of it—and I'm sure he knows it too. But he wants you to be quite certain."

"Jenny, I *am* certain! It's only—"

"Your parents? Haven't you tried to sound them out a bit?"

"No," said Clare, much subdued. "I've been so afraid that they might—oh, laugh at me or something. You're so lucky in a way, having only your mother, you know. Sometimes a family can be stifling. You see, he's been their friend for years, he's part of the scenery. It would seem so sudden of me to declare a grand passion for good old Edward."

"I don't see why." Families were a terrible complication, Jenny thought. They took away one's individuality and freedom. Nice to have around sometimes if they were like the Morleys, but a stumbling-block when it came to romance.

69

If it weren't for Charles Langton's family, for instance. . . .

"Anyway," Clare was saying, "I'm being a hog, as usual, going on about me. More to the point, my dear, you have made a great impression on the Earl."

"What?"

"He came into the Print Room when Edward was there. Asked all sorts of questions about you—how old you were, what school you went to, were your parents artists and so on—and then informed Edward that you could draw like an angel! Not bad, dear girl! You've hardly been here a week, and conquered the Earl already." Clare rolled over on the bed and fixed her with a penetrating eye. "What do you think of him?"

"Oh—" Jenny floundered. "He's nice," she said lamely.

"Nice! There's an epithet to thrill a girl's heart! No, seriously—what do you think?"

Jenny found it hard to control her voice. She and Clare had seldom kept secrets from one another—there had been none to keep, their short-lived passions had usually been simultaneous and shared. But now she felt quite incapable of explaining her tangled feelings about Charles Langton.

"He's—impressive," she said at last. "Utterly charming, as people with his kind of background usually are—but not very happy. That's what I think."

Clare nodded to herself.

"Interesting. You'll see the Lady Amelia tonight."

"The Lady Amelia?"

"Current candidate for next Countess of Langton. His mother's idea. Suitable pedigree, good looks and oodles of cash. The odds are heavily in favour."

"Oh." Jenny felt sick. Somehow she had not contemplated this eventuality. But of course it made no difference to her; how could it? So there was no reason why she should suddenly feel so cold, so thoroughly defeated. "It sounds like a very good idea," she said miserably.

"But you don't fancy the match."

"Whatever makes you think so?"

"The fact," said Clare, "that you look exactly like the martyred Sebastian contemplating all those nasty sharp arrows. Come off it, girl! You've fallen quite hard for the Earl, haven't you?"

"Yes," admitted Jenny, with a feeling of relief at being able to say so, at not having to pretend any longer. "But I'm not letting myself take it seriously."

"Why not?"

"Oh, Clare—need you ask? Me and an ermined Earl?"

"He's a very democratic Earl," said Clare, staring abstractedly at the bed-cover and picking at it with restless fingers. "Of course, everyone falls for him. It's the done thing, you know—you have to go through it, rather like the measles. But most people recover after a while, when the unreality of it strikes them. D'you think you will?"

"I'm not even certain that I'm very much in love with him."

"I don't see what else you could call it."

"Infatuation, maybe. Fascination. I don't know."

"Bad enough." Clare sighed. "If it's as involved as that, it isn't going to vanish overnight, is it?"

"Then I shall just have to ignore it and carry on as usual. Don't worry, Clare. I shan't embarrass you or let you down. I don't mean to make a spectacle of myself over him. But it's only just hit me, you see. Maybe I'll feel quite differently by morning."

Clare shot her a sceptical look.

"Some hopes! Oh, Jenny—it may be painful, but isn't it interesting? Much better to be in love than not, even if it hurts quite desperately—which of course it does, if it's the real thing. Here's me and Edward, you mad about Charles, and John—poor John, so much in love with Rowena, and so little hope!"

"If he's no hope, why should you think me any better off?"

"Dear thing, it matters much more the other way around. I mean, an earl can marry anyone—they frequently do—and she becomes a countess. But Lady Rowena would be descending to plain Mrs. Morley, wouldn't she? The old woman would have apoplexy."

"The Dowager Countess, you mean? Does it really all depend on her, then?"

"Very largely. Her grip is like steel—especially on Rowena. You'll understand when you've met them."

And Jenny did understand. The party from Morleys drove up the hill to the castle so as not to spoil fragile shoes or the hems of long dresses. It was a silvery night, the moon high and full, gilding the castle and making it unreal like something out of a fairy tale. Jenny sat very still in the car beside John and Clare, and felt a state of dreaming creep up on her. None of it was really happening; it wasn't herself here, perfumed and wrapped in silk, but some imagined creature, and the people with her were as unreal as she, driving further and further into her dream.

The Great Hall was rich with light and colour, and smelled of flowers. The pillars all were garlanded with hyacinths and jasmine, and great star bursts of daffodils decked the tables and made a bower of the stairs. When the party from Morleys had divested themselves of coats and wraps, there was the long walk up the stairs to be faced. Jenny surveyed herself in the cloakroom mirror first, feeling oddly detached from the image she saw. Her hair was taken up into a neat twist on top of her head, and there were flowers tucked into it, trembling little white lilies picked from the garden. Her face was pale and grave, with enormous dark eyes. She might have been Natasha Rostov, going to the ball to meet Prince Andrei; even her white dress suggested it, very much in the Empire style, with a pale green ribbon at the high waist and delicate embroidery at the hem.

"You look like a very young Jane Austen heroine," said Clare, coming to stand at her shoulder. "Beside you, I'm a very full-blown rose." She had dressed in shades of ivory and pink, layers of chiffon giving an impression somehow of petals and fragrance and softness. The golden swathes of her hair were coiled

and plaited into submission and yet still exuber-
antly curled as if struggling to be free. If Edward
Channing were able to remain silent tonight,
thought Jenny, then he was not worth having. But
he could not. Clare's fate must be settled before the
evening ended—though her own future was hidden
from her in darkness and despair.

Meekly they walked behind Mrs. Morley out into
the Great Hall, and there were joined by Leonard
Morley and John for the long ascent of the bowery
stairs. People were arriving minute by minute,
castle guides and estate workers unrecognisable in
evening splendour; a crowd seemed to surround
them as they moved up the long stairs. When they
turned at the half landing the reception line became visible, and Jenny felt her heart begin to
beat painfully fast, and she ached with nervous-
ness. Charles, Lord Langton, stood immaculate in
white tie and tails, his thick fair hair just unruly
enough to be utterly disarming; and beside him
were three women, at the sight of whom Jenny felt
immediately defeated. There was the dowager
first, small and ramrod straight, with a delicate
china-doll face and eyes like granite. Then came
a creature of such haughty, raven-haired beauty
that Jenny knew her at once for the future Countess of Langton, and could not imagine how ever
she had thought herself able to compete. They did
not even inhabit the same world, she and this com-
manding woman.

Last, and with Edward Channing close by her
elbow, stood a slight and pretty blonde, small-

featured and with a look of singular sweetness that somehow echoed yet wholly differed from her brother's more incisive countenance. Rowena, thought Jenny—and yes, she could see why this girl was so easily dominated by that small termagant of a mother. She could see also why John Morley loved her.

Save for Jenny there was no need of introductions. She at last was formally presented to the Earl by Mrs. Morley, and then by him to his mother, Lady Amelia and Lady Rowena. He did it all with a charming gravity, and yet reserved for her a special smile seeming to convey private amusement which he knew she would share. She had come armed against him, and at once she was lost. There was no defence against those grey eyes, no protection from his smile. It was all she could do to turn a properly deferential face upon the Dowager Countess and to return her greeting with equanimity.

But she quickly became sober, meeting the Countess's eyes. They were stony grey and cold.

"Ah, yes," the formidable little woman said. "The girl who draws so well. Such a pity we have you with us for so short a time."

There was no warmth in the words. Jenny felt indicted for drawing so well that she had attracted the Earl's attention by it. Moving on to take Amelia's hand, and looking into a face that was a mask of chill indifference, she became sure that she was marked down for special displeasure. It was a relief to turn to Rowena, who greeted her with genuine friendliness and interest, and clearly knew all about her already. Jenny felt astonished that the other two women could have been so much impressed by the Earl's passing interest in her that they should feel it necessary to greet her so coldly. Did they really believe themselves in danger of losing him to a peasant girl?

They had no need to worry. Away from him, and led into the first dance by John Morley, she armed herself anew. It was an occasion and a situation potent enough to turn any girl's head, but precisely because it was so she must be on her guard against letting a dream carry her away. He was not for her. Desirable, charming and even admirable he might be, but she could desire and admire only from a distance. For the summer would end, and with it her small part in his world. She didn't belong, and must not covet anything she found there—even love.

Six

The ballroom was white and gold and very beautiful. In Jenny's imagination it seemed just like a setting for the ball at which Natasha met her Prince Andrei. Somehow that book was always in her head; the atmosphere was so right, a mingling of splendour and feudalism, romance, and despair, and everywhere the delicate fluttering of silks and satins, the warm softness of perfumed skin, the glitter of jewels, a profusion of femininity against which the men appeared almost military in the strict black and white of evening attire. In long mirror walls the dancing couples whirled and swayed into infinity down gold-edged corridors under the crystal foliage of endless chandeliers. It all looked quite as unreal as it felt.

Jenny found herself well provided with partners, a whole succession of them as different from one another as it was possible to be, from the distinguished Edward Channing through the Langton family's doctor to the labourers from the estate. They were all likeable and amusing—but none was the partner she longed for. He had danced with his mother and with Rowena, and more than once with the Lady Amelia, and then he had embarked on a dutiful tour of the room, as amiable and charming to one as to the next. Out of the corner of her eye she watched him, and wondered if it would ever be her turn. As a worker on the estate she hardly counted, and as a stranger who had managed already somehow to incur his mother's displeasure she was more likely than not to be avoided. She tried to put him from her mind.

As so often in life, her moment came when she was least expecting it. John Morley had brought her a glass of champagne, and she was standing with him to drink it, laughing at something absurd he had said and yet filled with sympathy for him because his eyes were all the time searching after Rowena, and she knew all too well how he must feel.

"You have an enviable talent for collecting quite the prettiest girls, John," said Langton's voice, amused. "May I steal this one just for a while?"

She caught a glint of laughter in John's eye, as if he had been expecting such an approach. But she didn't care; she turned, and was in Charles Langton's arms, and reality ceased to exist.

She had never danced before with feet that seemed not to touch ground. She was unaware of them, conscious only of his nearness, his arms about her, his breath cool against her flushed cheek. He seemed to hold her very close. The world was a blur of flowers and music, the white and gold dazzle of the ballroom and the wide, shining mirrors.

There seemed to be no need to talk. Only presently he asked: "Did you finish the drawing?"

"Not quite," she admitted, "but I shall."

"Please."

And then again, at one point he murmured: "I wonder why I'd never heard of you?"

"But why should you?"

"Oh—I know Clare. And I thought I knew her friends."

"I'm rather a distant friend. Geographically speaking, that is."

"That must be the reason."

He seemed then to hold her even closer. And when the music ended he kept her hand, saying nothing, but waiting for the next dance. She wanted it to go on for ever, his arms about her and his heart beating so close, so very close to hers. But presently the music once more came to an end, and this time he gently led her back to where John was standing, and gave her into his keeping. It wasn't necessary to say anything; she read in his eyes all that she wanted to see, and knew that he too had experienced at least something of the closeness she had felt, the rightness in their being together, the magic of dancing without the need for words.

All through the rest of the evening traces of their magic lingered. Jenny was all but unaware of what partners she danced with; they seemed wooden, leaden-footed, and yet it didn't matter, she hardly saw them, but circled the floor soft in their arms and happy. It was unreasonable to feel so, but she could not help herself. John danced with her sometimes, and then she was filled with sympathy, knowing what he must feel; she had seen him dance with Rowena, but he danced more often with her. It pleased her that she was able to throw dust into prying eyes, both on her own account and on his; they were one another's alibi. Even in the early hours, when the last dance came, she was not too downcast when Charles Langton took the Lady Amelia in his arms, and she was still with John.

It was fine enough out of doors for them to walk home through the park. John seemed to need someone to talk to and Jenny felt like walking, the night was so gentle, the air laden with the warm scents of spring. They made their way round the huge, dark bulk of the castle, and wandered hand in hand slowly down the avenue towards Morleys, stopping now and again to let a noisy car pass, or to look back at the lighted windows now vanishing one by one as rooms were closed for the night and castle inmates went to bed. Jenny wondered in which room Charles was, what he was feeling, whether he thought at all of her.

"I like Rowena," she confided to John. "Clare told me about it—I hope you don't mind?"

"Of course not. I'm sure you're a very safe person to tell—and I know that Clare would find it difficult to keep a secret from you. She and Edward disappeared together, didn't they?"

"Yes. D'you think he's finally proposed?"

"If he hasn't, then I shall have something to say to him tomorrow," said John decidedly. "It's high time

Clare was settled, and he's quite the best thing for her. I like the fellow enormously."

"But Clare was worried about your parents' approval."

"I don't think she need have done. Granted, there's the age gap, but I don't think it will weigh too heavily against his many virtues. It's so obviously an ideal match."

"And what about you, John?" she ventured. "Could it really not be as straightforward between you and Rowena?"

"All rather sickening, isn't it?" His voice was bleak. "Of course it ought to be straightforward, in this day and age—it ought to be possible for the girl to marry anyone she chooses."

"But isn't it, really? I mean, if she insisted—I can't imagine that Lord Langton would oppose it, if he knew."

"I don't believe he would. Only I don't at the moment want to put the burden on him. It's too close to the heart of his own problem. Imagine it, Jenny—on the one hand his thinking is thoroughly up to date and even liberal—he knows he has this great debt to society which he must pay in all sorts of ways, by letting the public into the castle, by employing as many people as he can, by farming super-efficiently. And yet he is still a member of a ruling class, an aristocracy which exists, however much one may dislike the idea. Umpteenth in line of succession to the throne, and all that. He can't shrug off the past—the tradition, you know, of continuing the line and ensuring that future generations are equally aware of their duty. He could have married several times, but he hasn't done so, and I think it's because he can't make up his mind about the future—where the family's going, and the importance of blue blood and all that. He's trapped by indecision. So how can I face him with the problem of Rowena's marriage before he's got his own sorted out?"

Jenny was silent. The night wind seemed suddenly to blow chill about her shoulders.

"You think, then, that he'll marry for duty rather than for love?" she asked at last.

"I fear he may. But I hope he won't, because having decided against it for himself he could hardly insist on it for Rowena."

"Of course," she said in a small voice, "there's always the chance that love and duty will eventually coincide."

"Someone like Amelia, you mean? She's very ornamental, but I can't detect any sign of a grand passion—not on his side, at any rate. Of course she has his mother's backing, and that counts for a great deal."

"His mother seems a very determined little lady," said Jenny.

"Oh, she is. Porcelain with a core of steel—and an expert in the application of emotional blackmail. That's how she holds Rowena. No doubt it also affects him."

Jenny felt all the magic of the evening rapidly

drain away. Her feet were in contact with the ground again, and it was very hard. She walked on with John in silence, glad of the comfort of his hand on hers, closer to him than he knew in the shared bond of suffering. For a moment she even contemplated telling him the truth about her own feelings, but pride kept her tongue still—pride, and a vivid sense of the absurdity of her position, a Cinderella lovesick for a prince she could never hope to capture.

Presently they reached Morleys, and found Leonard and Mrs. Morley drinking Horlicks in the kitchen. Soon afterwards Clare arrived accompanied by Edward Channing, and radiant. She tugged Jenny away from the others and up to her room, and there divulged the very evident fact that Edward had proposed. He was to speak to her father later that same day.

"I'm so happy, I feel as though I could die of it!" she declared, "It's not a comfortable feeling, Jenny—I always thought it would be, but it isn't, it's terribly precarious, because I know I've done nothing to deserve such happiness."

But it wasn't a matter of deserving, Jenny thought, lying at last quiet in her own bed and watching the sky beyond the window grow pale. It wasn't at all to do with what one deserved or wanted or even needed—it was a matter of chance, the way the dice fell. For Clare the game had come out right. But for herself—she expected nothing, hoped for nothing from fate. There was no reason why she should. Events would take their own course regardless of her hopes or wishes, and she must resign herself to that knowledge and waste no more of herself on hopeless dreams.

It was hard, all the same, to get up in the morning and go over to the castle as usual, pretending that nothing at all had happened—even though the happening had been all in her mind. When she got there, it was to learn that the family had already gone to Tathwell.

"Up and away early, they were," the guide from the Long Gallery told her. "Seems her ladyship was impatient to go. Sick of the sight of paying public, she said—though I don't know where she thinks the money would come from, without them, to keep this great place going."

That was it, then. He had gone, and she might never see him again. Jenny tried hard to persuade herself that it didn't matter and that she would anyhow have got over it in a day or two, but the effort of pretending exhausted her. She was glad that Clare's happiness spread such a dazzle about them; it gave her cover, disguising her own silence and making any attempt at serious or extended conversation quite unnecessary.

The day belonged to Clare. Edward approached her father in the time-honoured tradition, and received his conditional consent, the condition imposed being a year's delay, to make quite certain of the steadiness of Clare's own feelings. It was generally agreed that this was fair—even by Clare herself, whose natural impulsiveness was on this occasion tempered by the realisation of the great importance of the step she was taking.

"I believe if I didn't love him so much, and weren't so sure, then I might very well chafe at the delay," she confessed to Jenny. "But it's all so right and inevitable that I can't. Though it will be hard— because he isn't the sort of man you leap into bed with unless the full might of church and law have said you may, and I do rather want to leap into bed with him."

Jenny resolutely shut her mind to any consideration of that sort where Charles Langton was concerned. It wasn't bearable. If she were once to begin to think of him in that way, she would have to go away from Langton; it wasn't possible to live so close to a man one desired, and not betray it. She had not known before—but then there were many things she had not known until now about loving and wanting; there were all the tormenting small memories, sudden images of grey eyes fringed with thick lashes, of his smile, the sound of his voice and the teasing way he spoke, or the feeling of his arms about her when they had danced—hackneyed things, she had read about them a dozen times, and yet she had never understood them until now, when she experienced for the first time the force of particular meaning generated by love.

It was much too late to pretend to herself that she was anything other than head over heels in love. But though she might admit the truth to herself, it would have been a different matter entirely to have to confess it to anyone else, and so she was glad of Clare's utter absorption in Edward which left her free from the fear of questions at least for that day. Somehow she managed to cover up the misery she was feeling. But the night was sleepless, and the next morning grey both in her head and in the sky beyond, a sullen day with a chill wind that fluttered the new small leaves on the trees in the park. After an early lunch she walked with Clare over to the castle. Eward was waiting for them in the Print Room. He greeted Clare with a kiss, and hugged her, and then turned to Jenny.

"Lord Langton was on the phone earlier," he said to her. "Something about some drawings you'd done, and his not having had time to look at them. He wants you to take them over to Tathwell."

"Heavens!" Her heart swelled and throbbed so violently within her that for a moment she could say nothing sensible. Colour rushed to her pale face and made it hot. "But how? I mean—"

"He's sending a car for you tomorrow morning." Edward smiled with an indulgent kind of amusement, almost as if he knew exactly how she felt. "He did say he hoped you wouldn't find the gesture too redolent of feudalism. You won't mind? I'm sure Clare will be all right here for the day, and if necessary I can always give her a hand myself."

"No, I don't mind." Jenny wanted to laugh; she felt ready to burst with the most hysterical joy, and yet she dared not betray what she felt. Besides, there was no cause for the elation surging through her— no real, sober cause for it. The gesture meant nothing—not even the small private joke Edward had passed on. It was nothing more than a mild pleasantry, acknowledging his amusement at her forthright views on privilege and power. He couldn't know how much the lordliness of his gesture in sending a car for her secretly thrilled her, making her feel somehow feminine and important to him, as if he really wanted her enough to have sent for her so.

She worried at it in her head for the rest of the day. He could after all have simply sent for the drawings; he could have asked Edward or anyone else to have taken them. Or he could have waited until his next visit to Langton. But he had sent for her. Of course, her commonsense urged, she could more easily be spared than Edward, her presence wasn't necessary to the smooth running of the castle. And as to the drawings—well, he might want them for some purpose. He might want to commission more, for new brochures, perhaps. There were all sorts of reasons why he could have sent for her, and none of them the right one.

Even Clare at last noticed her abstractedness.

"You really have got it rather badly, haven't you?" she observed when the Print Room for a while was quiet. "You're making me feel guilty."

"You said it was the done thing," Jenny defended herself. "Why should I be immune? There's no vaccination against it that I know of—nor any natural law to say that I shouldn't."

"But it's making you miserable. You are, aren't you?"

"Fairly, just at the moment."

"Oh dear!" Clare looked quite miserable herself. "I've been so selfishly wrapped up in me and Edward—"

"As so you should be!"

"But I haven't been keeping an eye on you. And now you've gone off the rails, and I don't know what to do about it."

"Leave me to find my own way back," advised Jenny. But she could not convince Clare that the solution was anything so simple, and Clare remained subdued.

That night Jenny tried to finish the drawing of the stone urn. She had not touched it since the day of the ball and found now that she could not see in her head what needed to be done to finish it. Too much of Charles Langton came between her and the paper. If she were to change it now, somehow she would have altered things between them, and she dared not do that. The sketch would have to go to Tathwell unfinished, like a symbol of her feelings for Langton himself—a way of telling him what she could not say in words. He would not understand, but that didn't so much matter. She would have told him the truth in a way that could hurt neither of them.

She was up early next morning and dressed with particular care, bearing in mind that at Tathwell she might encounter not only Charles, but his mother and his sister and the Lady Amelia too. After much thought she donned a silky brown dress and jacket which were in themselves quite subdued and yet became her particularly well, worn with an orangey silk scarf at the neck like a flag of defiance. Clare was unwillingly impressed.

"I think you ought to sail in scarlet from head to foot," she protested. "You do look very nice. But what he needs is to be thoroughly and determinedly seduced, not bargained with. You look too business-like for a temptress."

"I'm bearing in mind his mother," pointed out Jenny.

"Bother his mother! It's high time someone stood up to her." All the same Clare saw the force of the argument. The day was more likely to be peaceful, the less noticeable Jenny contrived to be. About the estate there were many tales told of girls who had been rash enough to incur the dowager's disapproval.

The car sent for Jenny was a large black Daimler. It purred along the lanes between Langton and Tathwell, and Jenny sat very upright in the back of it and tried not to feel quite so much like a village maiden selected for the lord's approval in the days of *droit du seigneur.* The very opulence of the vehicle seemed designed for such a situation. She felt small and vulnerable and lost in the cushioned depths of it, carried every moment nearer and nearer to a meeting with Charles Langton, and not knowing how she would face him when the moment came.

But after all it was not so very terrible. The car turned in at gates in a high brick wall and drove through a modest wood, coming to rest at last in front of a spreading, low house with white windows and a square white porch. It wasn't any grander than some of the country houses in Jenny's own village, though it was secluded and very beautiful, and the lawns about it were immaculate.

Charles Langton came out to meet her as she emerged from the car. In blazer and flannels, with a scarf knotted at his throat, he contrived to look every inch exactly what he was, an English country gentleman at home. Jenny thought back to their first meeting, and wondered now how ever she could have taken him for anything else. Such pleasure in seeing him rushed over her that all apprehension was lost; her hand went without hesitation into his, and when he smiled at her it was as if they were already lovers and understood without the need for words what her coming meant to both of them.

"I'm sure Edward didn't mind," he said. "Now he can spend all afternoon with Clare."

"It suits both of them very well."

"Then everyone's happy." He looked at her with an expression which seemed to invite her to take his words however she would. She longed to be able to do so, to believe that he had wanted her here for himself and had used the drawings as an excuse. But she dared not quite believe it.

"I didn't finish the drawing," she said, shaken by a sudden breathlessness. "I couldn't see what needed to be done."

"Perhaps there wasn't any more to be done, then. Come into the house and we'll see."

He ushered her in through open French windows,

to a long, low, cool room with pale green walls and a white fireplace, and fine Shiraz rugs upon the polished boards of the floor. There were a great many pictures on the walls, mostly watercolours, and none so large or striking as to clamour for attention or dominate the tranquillity around them.

Jenny looked about her with real pleasure.

"This is a lovely room," she said.

"Isn't it? To me the castle always feels rather like a large hotel, but this is home, it's our own place."

"Yes. I hadn't thought of it in that way." Most people took it for granted that one day they would go out into the world and choose a home of their own, however humble it might be; they would furnish and decorate it according to their own tastes and means. But a place like Langton Castle, with its very walls built of history, could never be that kind of a home.

"It's not an aspect of inheritance that strikes most people," he said. "They look at Langton and think how marvellous to own it all, and it doesn't occur to them that one might actually prefer quite a modest place in a village somewhere with congenial neighbors and a nice pub just down the road."

"Is there a nice pub down the road here?"

"Well, a quarter of a mile away—half, if you count the drive. But it's called The Earl of Langton."

"Oh dear!" But she shared in his amusement at his own fate, since he clearly did not take it too seriously.

"Now," he said, with an abrupt change of mood. "Show me the drawings."

She took them out of the folder in which she had been carrying them, and spread them on the polished rosewood table. He looked at them for a few moments in absorbed silence, so much intent upon them that she felt he had quite forgotten her.

"They really are very good," he said at last, as if he had half feared that they might after all not be, and was now more impressed than he had hoped. "Are they for sale?"

"Good heavens, no! I mean, you can have them anyway, but I don't want—"

"I wouldn't dream of letting you give them away. You're a professional artist, Jenny—and a good one. These are worth their market price. I shall instruct Edward Channing to make you an offer for them— we might as well do the thing properly, don't you think?—and I shall be very cross if you argue."

"But I didn't *intend*—"

"The intention was clearly purest art. That's why they're so good. But an artist can get pretty thin, you know, on pure intentions." He grinned at her. "Another good mark for my family, Jenny. Sometimes we have fed an artist for a week or two. Those pictures in the Long Gallery, you know— they were mostly commissioned, and all paid for."

Not for the first time she regretted some of the things she had said at their earlier meetings.

"You're really not kind!" she protested. "To keep throwing all that back at me, I mean. I never said you'd not paid. My only objection was to your being rich enough in the first place."

"But if we hadn't been, who else would have

bought the work of those artists? And there was no welfare state for them to fall back on. It was patronage or nothing."

She could find no answer. They seemed suddenly to be locked in a combat that was at least half serious, and she felt frightened and inadequate. She did not want to fight him. But he seemed to sense her reluctance, or perhaps to consider that round of the battle won, and he took pity on her.

"Come and see something of the house," he suggested. "The others have driven over to see friends, but they'll be back to lunch. There's a room set aside for you upstairs where you can leave your bag and so on; I'll get Mrs. Benson to show you up there first."

There was a bell-push by the fireplace, and he pressed it. Jenny, who had only ever seen this done in films, waited with an unwilling sense of awe to see who would appear. It turned out to be a very matronly lady, dressed exactly as a housekeeper should be dressed with touches of white at the collar and cuffs. At the Earl's bidding she took Jenny and showed her upstairs to the room made ready for her.

Seven

Tathwell was the sort of house Jenny had sometimes imagined for herself, indulging in fantasies of
the quieter kind. Despite its size it had simplicity
and a feeling of homeliness. The room set aside for
her upstairs was a charming country bedroom with
sprigged wallpaper and a half-tester bed, and a
small bathroom led from it. Out of the window she
could see over the gardens, beyond them a maze and
a tennis court and everywhere the misty green of
budding trees.

Of course, she argued stubbornly with herself,
only the very rich could afford to live in such
spacious simplicity. Its artlessness concealed re-
sources of a thoroughly solid kind. And yet against
her every objection Charles Langton seemed able to
raise a defence; he had them all by heart, but then no
doubt he had spent a lifetime defending himself.

It was all terribly unfair. She didn't know whether
to approve or disapprove, and hated the feeling of
having to pass judgement on him. Not that the
outcome was of the least importance to anyone else,
but to her it seemed to matter. She went downstairs

at last armed against him anew—and was almost at once as thoroughly disarmed.

He was the most charming companion imaginable. Showing her the drawing-room, dining-room, library, study and music-room, he was able to tell her brief histories of the furniture and pictures, and perhaps incidentally to offer her a great many glimpses into his childhood and the way his character had been shaped. The past coiled its tentacles about the present everywhere, even in this house. Yet the feeling of the place was right; it seemed to have achieved perfection without the least contrivance after effect.

"I suppose," she said, "the building up of a perfect interior is an art just as much as the painting of a picture."

"I think it is. And remember that it has to be lived in, not just looked at. So there's an extra dimension to the art."

"Have you ever lived anywhere ordinary?" she asked him. He looked sidelong at her, as if he suspected that the question might be meant to sting.

"I could reply that to me this seems quite ordinary," he said after a moment. "But I won't. I'll say instead that I have stayed with friends who live in cottages and flats, and I've lived in college rooms and school dormitories. And, d'you know, I managed to find something extraordinary in all of them."

"You mean that ordinariness is in the eye of the beholder?"

"I mean that I don't know what 'ordinary' means.

One man's ordinary is another man's poison, if you like."

He grinned at her with a charming boyishness that she found utterly devastating. One couldn't quarrel with him in this mood; not that she wanted to, really, but she was nagged at by the need to clarify her own confused and contradictory notions of what his world was really like. At the back of her mind all the time was an uneasy suspicion that the whole occasion had been laid on so that she might do just that. But if so, she did not understand why he should have thought it necessary. It seemed absurd that he should have gone to such lengths simply to put right the views and opinions of a chance and unimportant acquaintance, someone quite outside his own social sphere. It was conceited to imagine that she really mattered so much to him—conceited, and dangerous.

They strolled out into the garden, along paved paths edged with cushiony herbs, past a little lake, and eventually back to the maze, where Charles obligingly allowed her to lead the way and become hopelessly lost.

"It's a very simple maze," he said at last, when with great thought and a certain amount of cheating she had found the middle. There were seats on either side of a little pool, and they rested there for a few moments, shaded by the tall, dark yew hedges.

"Mazes are always simple when you know the trick," she retorted. He was sitting at the other end of the bench, his arm thrown over the back of it, watching her. She felt uncomfortably hot and bothered. "Anyway," she pointed out, "you'd have been disappointed if I hadn't got lost. That's what mazes are for, to get lost in."

"Perhaps they are." He seemed all at once to become detached, remote from her, as if he had suddenly remembered that after all she was hardly a friend of the family, but an employee to whom he was being uncommonly forbearing. "You don't much like the feeling of being lost, do you?" he observed then.

"Not very much. I prefer to know where I'm going."

"But you'd put up a fight all the same. You wouldn't panic or go to pieces."

"There's no point," she said. "I might panic inside. But I'd stay calm on the surface. There would be more chance of finding a way out then, wouldn't there?"

Suddenly they weren't talking about mazes any more, but about something much more profound. She felt that he was making a real effort to judge, to evaluate that aspect of her character, as though it mattered to him what stuff she was made of. She almost panicked then, and wanted to beg him to leave her alone because to encourage her was dangerous and she was already too much dependent on his opinion of her. But she could find no way to warn him; she had not his gift for making words say so much more than was in them.

"It's possible," he was saying now, "to get lost and not want to find one's way out. There are mazes like that, you know."

"Yes." She had difficulty in speaking. Her breath

would not come steadily, and an acute awareness of him, of being so utterly and privately alone with him, spread like a fire through all her limbs.

"What does one do then, Jenny?" he asked, and now there was no pretence that they were talking about anything but themselves—both knew it, and knew that the real issue was this fierce attraction between them.

"I don't know—what to do." She wanted to break away, to give way to the panic she had boasted of being able to resist. This was a kind of being lost she had never experienced before.

"I think," he said deliberately, moving along the seat until he was very close to her; "I think one gives in a little, don't you? Silly not at least to enjoy the adventure."

"If there's no help for it," she whispered.

"Is there, Jenny? Is there?"

"Oh, none," she moaned, and was in his arms, burying her fingers deep in the soft thickness of his hair. His lips met hers with such tenderness and with such passion that for a moment she thought she could not bear it; but even as she resisted, desire for him flared in her and made her pliant in his arms, yielding under the persuasion of insistent kisses.

"Jenny," he murmured, and again, "Jenny, Jenny," as if even her name were a delight to him. His lips moved from her mouth to the soft pulse beneath her jaw, and to her smooth, warm throat, and all the while she clung to him without thought of resistance, wanting him never to stop, her hands as if in a fever caressing his tousled, shiny hair.

"Oh, Jenny!" he murmured huskily against her throat. "You bewitch me. It seems forever that I've been lost in this maze of your making. Lost and tormented!"

A fierce kind of triumph filled her, to think she could make him want her so much. She held his head between her hands and forced him to look up at her. His eyes were dark and dazed with feeling, and there was pain in them. Perversely, it gave her pleasure.

"Oh," she cried, "I want to torment you! I want to give you no peace, as you give me none—I want you to want me more than anything—!"

His mouth silenced her then, imperious and demanding, and his hands began to move over her body, smoothing and stroking her as if she were some young animal to be caressed into submission, so that gradually she became aware of nothing save the need for him which sprang from deep within her, flowing out towards him in one great surging, reckless tide.

And then he stopped. He took her by the shoulders and put her away from him, sitting removed from her, breathing hard and looking at her warily.

"It's a dangerous game," he said unsteadily. "I wouldn't play it if I were you—not unless you're prepared to lose."

She felt bewildered, stricken. Her hands reached instinctively towards him and then fell back into her lap, agitated, trembling; her whole body ached and yearned for him.

"I don't understand!" she cried weakly. "It's not a game—Charles, truly, I didn't mean—"

"Oh, women never do. They bewitch, they tease, they ensnare—but of course they never mean it."

"Very well, then, I do mean it—if that's what you want. I don't know what it is you want." She was shaken to the edge of tears, not understanding him, not understanding herself. His face changed then; the frost in the grey eyes melted and was replaced by a kind of wonder, an unwilling belief.

"Jenny," he said, "you almost persuade me. The trouble is, I'm used to women of another kind. I'm used to defending myself. But if you are real—if what I see in you is true, then I've no defence against you. It frightens me a little. You must forgive me."

"I would, if I understood."

"Never mind." He reached out and drew her gently against him so that her head rested on his shoulder. With a kind of wonder he stroked the smooth fall of her dark hair.

"The truth is," he said, "I don't any longer recognise simplicity or innocence. I so rarely meet them. There are women, Jenny, who would trade themselves in return for the Langton title—but never honestly. Always with a pretence at love. Sometimes I've thought it might be best to advertise the position, you know, with hours and conditions of work, so that at least I'd know where I stood. But you seem—different. And if I let myself believe you, I would give you the power to hurt me. D'you see?"

She lay for a moment quiet against his shoulder, feeling the strong beating of his heart under her hand, the warmth of his breath on her temple. She thought that she began to understand.

"But I wouldn't hurt you," she said simply. "Not ever."

"That's a reckless promise. Do you really think you ought to make it?"

"I want to. All right—I suppose two people can never really say such a thing, because loving means laying oneself open to hurt, doesn't it? But I wouldn't ever want to hurt you, I wouldn't do it knowingly."

He held her a few moments more, silent, abstracted, as if far down within himself he were trying to come to a decision.

"I hadn't meant to plunge us in so deep," he said at last. "Not all at once. You leave me very breathless, Jenny."

"I'm sorry," she said in a small voice. "I didn't mean to throw myself at you."

"Oh, it's not that, you little goose! I only mean that—well, I wasn't prepared, I suppose, to feel so strongly myself. I hadn't realised how far it had gone. We've hardly met, have we? We know nothing about one another."

"Yes we do," she said. "You can be with someone years and still not know them. Or you can meet a person and know all that matters about them almost at once."

"Do you feel like that about me?"

"Yes."

He kissed her then, long and tenderly, and with a queer kind of despair.

"Oh," he said against her lips, "how you bewitch me! It's as well you mean me no harm. You could destroy me, Jenny—do you know that?"

She ought to have been frightened, but she could only feel a tender, triumphant indulgence, a great exaltation. It was the power of womanhood, and she knew it for the first time, and felt as if all the secrets of the world were open to her.

But he put her away from him at last, smoothing his ruffled hair, deliberately returning them both to normality.

"Really," he said, amused, "this won't do! It's not at all the behaviour of the ideal host. Besides, my mother and the girls will be back by now and may very well come to look for us."

His mother. Jenny had forgotten. A coldness grew in the pit of her stomach and the feelings of exaltation began to evaporate.

"Oh dear," she said, "I don't feel at all able—"

"You mustn't be afraid of her. She's too much used to getting her own way—she's been spoiled, that's the trouble. But you'll find that if you humour her, and quietly go your own way, there's no need to fight her."

Jenny wouldn't have dreamed of attempting to fight that steely little woman. But she did not say so. Obediently she tidied her hair and smoothed her rumpled dress. It was hard to look at Charles now without letting her feelings show.

"We'll talk again another time, and perhaps a little

more rationally," he said as they got up from the seat and began to stroll back through the tightly winding pathways of the maze. Her arm was drawn through his, and they were very close. Yet already she found it hard to believe that she had not imagined the scene just past. Perhaps he felt the same. Without the exaltation, she could see no further into his mind than before, and felt forlorn and insecure.

They came into the house, and found that the women had indeed returned and that luncheon was waiting for them. It was clear to Jenny from the outset that her presence met with no approval from the Countess, nor from Amelia. They were icily polite. But she was left in no doubt as to her standing in their world; she might have been one of the stable girls come into the house with muddy boots on, or some undesirable creature picked up by Charles Langton from the streets. Only Rowena was amiable, and that very quietly, as if she might be afraid to show too much friendliness in her mother's presence.

Jenny tried to take her cue from Charles, and behaved as though nothing at all were amiss. She made such conversation as she could, principally with him and Rowena, and pretended that she did not notice the way in which the Countess and Lady Amelia ignored her. It was hard, all the same, to swallow her pride and to restrain the occasional cutting remark that sprang to mind. She would have liked a chance to show them what she felt. But she sensed in Charles a growing, pent-up anger, and suspected that once she had gone she might be well defended. This eased a little the effort of holding her tongue and pretending to a meekness she did not feel.

A sense of profound unreality began to steal gradually over her. It was rather like finding oneself caught up in a scene from a play, a group of characters well spaced about a polished table on which silverware and crystal and spotless white napkins shone as if designed to be photographed in close-up. The conversation became every moment more stilted and contrived. Jenny could not relate it to herself or to those passionate few moments in the maze. She found herself wondering if it were all unreal, if somehow her desire for Charles Langton had taken over her mind and woven sick fantasies there. Presently no doubt she would come to her senses, reality would wrap her in its cold clutch, and she would find herself as far from knowing him as ever she had been. It wasn't possible that he could love her. Even supposing just for a moment that she were not dreaming, and that he really had held her in his arms and kissed her and said all those things—even so, he could not have meant by them at all what she so desperately wanted him to mean. Perhaps just in passing she did attract him. It was conceivable that he found her a little out of the ordinary—unlike the Lady Amelia, for instance, and so possessed of a certain novelty. But that wasn't what she wanted from him. She had no wish to be a season's brief diversion; she was headlong and wholly in love with him, and wanted him as deeply in love with her. Yet that was on the face of it quite impossible. He was the Earl of Langton, and she was nobody. His mother and Amelia, after all, had got it right.

That fact stuck like a hard lump in her throat and would not be swallowed. It remained with her when, after lunch, she went up to her room to tidy before setting out with Charles and Rowena on a brief tour of the estate. She was down before either of them, and went to wait out on the terrace, wanting to be out in the open air, feeling oppressed by the silent hostility of the house now that the Countess was at home in it.

There was a window standing open a few yards away from the place where she waited. Gradually she became aware of voices, and having once tuned in to them, could not fail to identify them. Nor could she avoid hearing what they said, such was the high-pitched clarity of their tone, floating out into the still air of the afternoon as though they did not care who heard them.

"He may feel the need for these tedious little exercises in democracy, but really I wish he wouldn't inflict them on us," the Countess remarked.

"Too boring for you," the Lady Amelia commiserated. "All the same, she seems harmless enough—or didn't you think so? Surely he can't be seriously interested?"

"Not seriously—heavens, no! Charles may be annoying, but he does possess a certain sense of what's fitting. A little diversion, perhaps—they do happen from time to time, you know. He's a man, after all. But sensible enough to keep these things separate from everyday life. One learns when to turn a blind eye."

"Does he make a habit of bringing them into the house? I shouldn't at all care for that."

"I don't think you need fear any such thing once you are established, my dear. Charles has quite good manners, under normal circumstances. I can't think what induced him to bring this girl here, but I'm sure, whatever it was, he will very quickly tire of it. A perfect nonentity, I thought her."

"I believe she can draw. Perhaps it's an act of patronage. He likes that, doesn't he?"

"Yes," said the Countess, and added drily, "particularly if the object of patronage happens to be a pretty girl."

"You thought her pretty?"

"In an anaemic, board-school sort of way. Did she not come to the Ball with John Morley?"

"So she did," recalled Amelia with some satisfaction. "So it may be—"

"If the girl has any sense—and I daresay she has a little, despite all that air of meekness—then she'll go for what's attainable and waste no time on Charles. It's so patently absurd, one wonders how some of these girls could ever imagine—"

"Perhaps they receive a certain encouragement."

"Oh, I'd have thought Charles would be honest with them. But one must allow for imagination and ambition, I suppose. And one can't expect them to understand his sense of obligation. It's outside of all the things they learn at school or afterwards."

Jenny could endure no more. Very quietly, terrified lest she betray her presence, she moved away from the window and further along the terrace. A chill breeze caught at her, ruffled her hair, cooled her burning face. She felt sick and wounded. It was bad enough to hear oneself discussed in that way, loftily dismissed as harmless, barely intelligent enough to perceive on which side one's bread was buttered—but what hurt more than anything was their assessment of Charles' involvement with her. A diversion, no more, and at that only one among many.

They knew him, of course, and she did not. She had judged him by the standard of her world, which wasn't his, and maybe they were far enough apart for the rules of one to have no validity in the other. She simply didn't know.

"A little diversion, perhaps—they do happen from time to time." The words seemed to hiss and echo in her head, deriding her. She had believed him when he spoke of her power to destroy him, she had thought him passionate and honest, and her response to him had been guileless and direct. But the strength of her own feelings perhaps had blinded her to reality, had made his avowals of love seem deeper than they were. Amelia and the Countess were hard as nails, but they were realists, and their view of the situation probably came nearer the truth than her own dazzled dream. There was no reason why he should love her just because she loved him, and every reason in the world why he should not.

Confusion and indecision numbed her so that

she could see nothing straight. By the time that Charles and Rowena came to join her on the terrace she had reached a kind of despairing calm, and went obediently with them to walk in the park and along the lanes of the estate. She made conversation without knowing or much caring what she said. Charles drew her hand through his arm and she let it lie passive there, unable to feel the least response in herself to his closeness or to whatever impulse had prompted his gesture. It was all rather like a dream—only not a happy dream this time, but frozen and dark, and touched with the horror of nightmare.

Eight

At the end of the afternoon it was the Countess who mentioned that John Morley was coming to fetch Jenny home.

"We have to dine out," she said, by way of explanation. "But I'm sure you must find young Morley most agreeable company, so I need not apologise."

And no doubt, thought Jenny, John had been glad enough of the chance to come over to Tathwell and perhaps to see Rowena. For her own part, she certainly would find his company pleasing. At least with John she knew where she stood, and his brotherly affection would be a refuge from the tensions and uncertainties of the day.

"Shall you be glad to see him, then?" Charles asked her *sotto voce*, and with a certain waspish irritability which had been growing on him all afternoon, as if perhaps he might be annoyed with himself for having got into so equivocal a situation.

"Yes, I shall," she declared rather more warmly than was quite wise. "I like John very much, he's a thoroughly genuine person. But then I like all his family."

"I see." His eyes strayed for a moment to Rowena, who sat over her embroidery by the window, some little way removed from them. "You find them—what was the word?—more ordinary, maybe."

He was harking back to her question that morning, when she had asked him if he had ever lived in an ordinary house. She remembered that he had replied that to him, Tathwell seemed ordinary. The memory unreasonably depressed and chilled her.

"If ordinary means friendly and kind, then yes," she replied. "But maybe you don't mean that."

"I only wonder what has been going on in your head all afternoon."

They were conducting their conversation in undertones, almost furtively, and apart from the others. Jenny felt angry that it should have to be so. She wanted to shout at him, to cry in anger: "This morning you made love to me, you awoke in me feelings I hadn't known existed, you made me believe you. And then I found out the truth. I found out what your mother and your wife-on-approval thought about it, and now I don't know what to believe any more. That's what's been going on in my head all afternoon."

But somehow the silent room smothered such utterances. There was an atmosphere of icy rectitude, and she had not the courage to break it.

"I've had time to ask myself some questions," she said quietly. "There's been time for me to think a little more realistically."

"I see." His grey eyes were bleak. "A change of heart, perhaps?"

"I don't know, Charles—I don't *know!*" Her voice had risen, and in a sudden panic she heard it, and at once bit back all the rest of what she might have said.

"Well," he murmured, "I did confess that I hadn't meant to plunge us in so deep. Maybe it's just as well. I'll remember, in future."

"Oh, please—" She longed then to erase the bitterness from his face, to melt the ice in his eyes, but she could find no words to say what her heart ached with. There was no time to search for the means to tell him; John was almost at once announced, and she found herself politely but firmly handed over to him and dismissed from the premises as rapidly as the minimum of courtesy allowed.

Charles and Rowena saw them to the car. The evening had begun to be cold, the sun obscured by a bank of cloud, and Jenny shivered, huddling into the seat beside John and looking out at brother and sister standing on the lower step of the terrace. There was a great similarity between them. Both looked at that moment bitterly-unhappy, and seeing that likeness, Jenny longed to reach out to him, to cry that it had all been a misunderstanding and that she loved him no matter what. But the bleakness in his eyes warned her of the folly of such reckless declaration. Just now, certainly it would be rejected. He was angry; no doubt his pride had suffered, and maybe there was bewilderment too—she must at first have seemed a conquest so easily won.

Elaine Daniel

As the car pulled away her eyes were blurred with tears. She ached for comfort.

"You survived, then," commented John from the driving seat beside her.

"Just about. But only just."

"The Dowager Countess?"

"To be frank, the lot of them. Excluding Rowena, I suppose—though honestly, John, I'd think more of her if she showed a little more spirit. They let the old woman get away with murder."

"Not always. Charles doesn't."

"He conceals his resistance well, then."

"He doesn't so much resist as ignore. But I'm sorry you've had a rough time. I wouldn't have thought Charles would allow it."

"Maybe it was my own fault. I didn't play the right game. I'm not very sure what game I was supposed to be playing." Her head throbbed, and she closed her eyes in an effort to hold back the tears. "They're a species all on its own; it's better not to get involved with them," she said. She sensed rather than saw John's sidelong glance.

"Yes," he agreed after a moment. "Non-involvement is the best policy, no doubt about it. Anyway, it's back now to the comparative peace of Langton without them. Your nerves will soon recover."

She wished that she could believe him. But she felt as if her whole body had been put through some vast, impersonal breaking machine, with her mind all the while trapped inside it. Silly, to react so strongly to the common or garden process of mak-

112

ing a fool of oneself. She suspected that she had come perilously near to making a public spectacle of herself over Charles Langton. Perhaps she ought after all to be grateful to his mother and Amelia for saving her at the last moment.

She had left Morleys that morning in a state of mingled exaltation and apprehension. She returned sober and cold. Clare met her at the door, fizzing with questions, and there was no simple answer she could make to any of them.

"It was all rather trying and confusing," she confessed at last, when they were safe in her room and she was changing out of the suit she had worn for the day. "He was charming some of the time, frosty at other times, and his mother was a solid icicle." There was no point in telling Clare what had really happened. She could not have explained it, nor even have found words—and besides, it hurt, it was the kind of private wound that goes too deep for sharing. She felt ashamed of what had taken place that day.

"He wanted to buy the drawings," she said. "That was the real reason for the visit."

"Tosh! He could have done that at any time—or got Edward to do it for him."

"Well—maybe he thought me in need of a day out to see how the other half lives. One of the under-privileged, you know."

"I don't in the least believe it," said Clare decidedly. "I'd quite made up my mind that he was definitely interested in you—and I still think it. Why otherwise such a King Cophetua kind of gesture? Only maybe—oh, maybe that awful mother of his got at him, or—"

"If he's so easily deflected, then he really isn't very worth while, is he?" pointed out Jenny. "No, Clare—it's all soap bubbles, pretty but hardly practical. I've been a fool to let myself fall for him, but not such a fool as to think there's anything in it for me. You'll see—I'll have got over it in no time at all, probably establish the Estate speed record and be spoken of with awe for ever after."

She spoke lightly because there was no other way she dared to speak. Weeping was for later, when she lay alone in her bed; then she was able to go over it all at leisure, examining each look, each remembered word in a miserable search for reassurance. But there was no comfort to be found in any of them. A dangerous game, he had called it—and she, not understanding, had protested that she played no game. But now she understood him well enough.

A week went by, and another. The daffodils withered and died, the trees became heavy with green. In the Castle gardens a riot of thick blossom made masses of colour and soaked the air with fragrance under a cloudless sky.

The Castle became much busier. At weekends so many visitors came that the halls and vaulted corridors resembled nothing so much as a huge railway terminus, echoing to the calls of voices and the shuffling of feet. During the week there were school parties and foreign tourists, so that there was no time when the place was really quiet until the last of the visitors had gone and the great iron-studded doors were closed after them. Jenny was glad to be busy, since it left less time for thinking.

Edward Channing duly presented himself to her one day with the Earl's offer for her drawings. It was a larger sum than she had expected, but on reflection she found it nicely judged—it was neither so extravagant an offer as to make her feel patronised, nor so mean as to suggest that he was willing to take advantage of an artist as yet unknown. Briefly she considered refusing it, insisting that he keep the drawings for nothing as an indication that they meant nothing to her. But it would be foolish to let pride stand in the way of legitimate profit. She was an artist, after all, and her work was worth whatever price a buyer might be prepared to offer. Besides, once the summer ended she still had to live.

She accepted his money, and by doing so seemed to make the gulf between them wider than ever.

These days, despite the never-ending stream of visitors, the castle seemed somehow empty. Sometimes, before the doors were opened to the public, she would go and stand before the Hoppner portrait of the tenth Earl. From the very start she ought to have read the lesson so glaringly evident in that bold, handsome, self-willed face. There were already generations of privilege bred into the bone; it wasn't the face of a tender or a loving man—nor even an honest one, unless to be quite frank about one's ruthlessness were to be honest. And yet . . . she could not forget grey eyes smiling into hers, the rueful tilt of lips half apologetic, self-mocking, amused. She could not forget his voice husky with the force of feeling, his words that had almost stammered from the sincerity with which they were spoken.

It was a conflict she did not know how to resolve. The tension exhausted her, pulling her first this way and then that, giving her no peace by day or night. Every morning she rode with the Morleys and swam in the castle pool, every evening was taken up by visits to other homes on the estate or walks with John or riding again, but all the time inside herself she struggled to understand, and longed for reconciliation with the only man whose company really mattered.

So the long summer days slowly passed by. There was talk of the family moving from Tathwell down to London, of their calling at Langton *en route*, of an engagement between Lady Amelia and the Earl. Rumours, said Clare, dismissing them. And nothing happened.

It was rather like a Chekov play, Jenny thought; people elegantly and aimlessly circling one another, passing away the endless summer in a kind of dream. But it was more pleasant than Chekov, and certainly more energetic. She had learned to ride with a competence that surprised and pleased her. Long ago now she had graduated from the staid gelding on whose broad back she had begun, and galloped the long rides over the park on Millamant, a lovely chestnut mare whose quality even she had grown knowledgeable enough to appreciate.

She loved riding. The movement, the exhilaration and effort released tensions that otherwise would have seemed unbearable. And afterwards she enjoyed rubbing down and grooming the glossy hide of the creature; somehow the smell of stables, the clatter of hooves and the large presence of the horses comforted her in a way that people could not. Of all the things she would miss about her life at Langton this would leave the greatest gap—apart always from the one bereavement for which nothing could ever console her.

John and Clare were her companions on morning rides, and sometimes Edward Channing too. On one such morning, they had left the park and gone out into the country, meandering in hot sunshine beside fields of slowly ripening corn, down into the Vale of Langton and back again by ancient drove roads, board green lanes between high and shady hedges. John rode beside Jenny, leaving Clare and Edward to loiter blissfully behind them.

"The land looks thoroughly contented," Jenny remarked at one point. "As though it's doing what it was meant to do and somehow knows it."

"Which is another way of saying it's well farmed," John said. "I imagine there are few bits of England better tended."

"Is it really all Langton territory?"

"Almost as far as you can see. It justifies the system, don't you think? You couldn't imagine that it would be better farmed as some kind of people's collective, or whatever."

"No," said Jenny in a small voice. "I've given up that notion. The system of land-ownership may be unfair, but it works."

"Life is unfair, Jenny. It is, you know. People may think they can change it, make it fairer, but in the end they can't—because no one can control all the factors, whether they're born brainy or beautiful or what accidents may arise, sickness, mistakes—all these complications are outside our control."

"Like you wanting Rowena," she said, and thought, like me wanting Charles. I can't have him because life unfairly made him rich and me poor; because he belongs to another class, because one set of values makes sense to him, and another to me.

"You must admit," John was saying, "that Langton pays his debt. He fulfils all the obligations laid on him by privilege."

"There was a rumour—" The words came painfully; it was hard to say them with indifference, as though they did not hurt her. "People were saying that he and Amelia might announce their engagement quite soon."

"Well—" John shook his head. The horse, sensing his movement, swerved and for a moment was restive. "I don't know," he said when the creature was steady again. "I'll believe it when it happens. Rowena hasn't said anything in her letters. If he does marry Amelia it will be the ultimate in *noblesse oblige*—probably the last grand gesture of its kind that England will ever see, barring the Royals, of course, who have the most difficult path of all to tread."

"He may actually care for her, of course." There were many different ways of caring; she could dimly understand an attachment quite other than love, which yet might make a strong foundation for marriage.

"Possibly he does," said John. "But Langton's a man who needs real red-blooded love, not a cool kind of caring. He's a deep sort of fellow. I could imagine him positively reckless, were he ever to give himself a long enough rein. But without love he'll shrivel and dry up into a desiccated caricature."

His words stirred in Jenny the most disturbing and painful sensations. Unable to bear them she urged Millamant to a trot and then to a canter, and called back to him, "Race you to Morleys!" Behind her she heard the thudding hoofbeats of his horse. They were almost at the boundary of the park; there was a post and rail fence, and she set Millamant at it and cleared it with a great, heart-throbbing jump which sent her crashing back into the saddle, clinging on for dear life and half laughing, half crying at her own recklessness. But the mare was equal to anything. She surged over the park, up the steep slope to Morleys, and arrived with a great clattering of hooves in the stable yard. There she stopped, panting and curvetting with delight at her own effortless prowess, with Jenny limp and trembling in the saddle.

John was close behind her into the yard. He dismounted and came to her, admiration not unmixed with anger.

"You could have broken your neck!" he cried,

reaching up to help her down. "I've never been so frightened in my life."

She slid down into his arms and clung to him, her legs shaking so that for a moment they would not hold her.

"Oh, John, I've been over jumps before." She smiled up at him, aware that her lips were trembling and her eyes wet with tears. Fiercely he hugged her.

"Damned idiot!" he swore. "A jump in the field's one thing, but a solid post and rail fence nearly five foot high . . .!" He turned to the group of people standing in the yard of whose presence she had been only dimly aware.

"Clear over the fence at the bottom of the park!" he declared, not without a certain element of pride. "And made it look like nothing at all. If she could do it in the show ring she'd be a world-beater."

She lifted her head from his chest and pushed herself a little away from him, looking at them against the dazzle of the sun.

"All in all," said a familiar voice drily, "I'd rather she didn't take her teething fences on one of the better horses."

Jenny felt all the warmth drain out of her. She had heard of people turning suddenly to stone, and had thought it a somewhat fanciful expression, but now she experienced it for herself; her body seemed oppressed, weighed down with coldness.

"I'm sorry, Lord Langton," she said through stiff lips. "I didn't stop to think. Millamant wanted to go over the fence, so—we went."

The Lady Amelia was on his arm. They were

dressed for riding, and the grooms were leading out two horses. Amelia regarded Jenny with a kind of tolerant amusement; she looked unfairly beautiful in a riding hat, a silk bandeau confining her hair, the ends of it fluttering in the faint breeze. Jenny felt grubby and untidy, her face flushed from the ride, her hair wild under her hat. And John Morley's arms were clasped about her still, as if he were afraid to let her go.

She tried to break away from him, but he would not entirely release her.

"Really," he was saying to the Earl, "she can ride. We'd never have given her Millamant otherwise. And it's the first even remotely reckless thing she's ever done, I can vouch for that."

"Can you?" Langton sounded grimly amused. His eyes met Jenny's, and there was a kind of challenge in them. "It can be dangerous, all the same, to give way to a reckless impulse—especially if you lack the courage to follow it through. I'd be more careful, if I were you. Or more committed."

He turned away from her then, and easily mounted the horse brought for him. Amelia was helped up by the groom; in a moment they were gone into the sunlit park, and neither of them looked back.

Jenny leaned helplessly against John. Her whole body was shaking; she wanted to laugh and cry, to rage against the unfairness of the world, to weep for the bitterness of it. John held her comfortingly close.

"It's all right," he said. "He didn't mean it. Millamant's not really one of the string—she's a good

ride, but not a blood horse. He was—well, teasing
you, don't you think?"

"Yes," said Jenny. "That's it. Teasing me." But
cruelly, in a way that John could not possibly
understand. It was the charge of cowardice that
hurt the most. He had flung in her face the fact of
her own timidity—the fact that she had let herself
become confused, had not held on to him through
the bewilderment and self-doubt of that day at
Tathwell. It hurt, because he was right. She had
tried to play too big a game, and had lost her nerve.
And so, she supposed, she had hurt him. He had a
right to his anger.

She let the groom take Millamant, and allowed
John to support her back to the house. There she
soaked in a bath, and tried to believe that she could
so easily soothe away the pain of encountering
Charles. But it remained stubbornly with her. The
fact was that he had offered her, that day at
Tathwell, a relationship of some kind—love, maybe,
or an affair, an involvement—something. And she
had seemed at first to accept it, and then capricious-
ly to reject it. He could not know her reasons. He
couldn't know the insecurity, the self-doubt—nor
the effect of that overheard conversation between
his mother and Amelia. He was used to women of a
tougher kind, women who knew what they wanted
and went single-minded after it. There was no way
he could have understood her motives.

It wasn't going to be possible for her to stay on at
Langton. That had become quite clear to her. She
could not bear the place any longer; it was too full of

him, too resonant with her own failure. She made up her mind that she would tell Clare and Edward this very afternoon, and then go—before it was too late. He had said that she had the power to destroy him. Clearly she had not done so; he was surviving very well without her. But nothing had been said about his destroying her. If she stayed, it would happen; she could feel already the chilly death of hope, the cold encroaching shadows of life without him. Her only chance lay in removing herself, in going right away and making herself forget him somewhere where she would not constantly be reminded. Coward she might be, and irresolute, but she would fight with every atom of strength she had to be free of him at last. But it could not be done at Langton. She had to get away.

Nine

Clare was devastated by the news that Jenny meant to leave Langton.

"But the season's only half over, and there's the riding and all the fun of summer! Jenny, you can't mean that this thing about the wretched Earl has you beaten. You'll be running away!"

"That's exactly what I'll be doing. Running for my life."

"But—they may not come back for weeks. You might never see him again—not until the Corn Ball, anyway. And you wouldn't be forced to go to that."

It was impossible to make Clare see that to be at Langton and not go to the ball would be worse even than going to it. Jenny had run out of words; there was no way she could explain.

"Langton is him," she said simply. "The place is his past, his family. He's made of Langton. I just can't bear to be here. I'm bitterly sorry—I don't want to leave you or John or your parents, I don't want to miss the riding or swimming or parties—but I simply can't bear to be here. I must get right away and not be reminded of him. Think how you'd feel if it were Edward, if your parents had forbidden the marriage—"

But Clare, whose love was uncomplicated and direct, could not imagine it. She would have wanted to remain near her man whatever the cost; his presence, the daily reminders of his existence, would have been a comfort to her and not a torment. But then, between her and Edward there had never arisen such bitterness as had sprung out of that ill-fated day at Tathwell.

John was more easily able to understand.

"It's the Earl, isn't it?" he asked her, when she had told him that she must go. "I've been somewhat obtuse, I'm afraid, not seeing how far it had gone. If you want to tell me—"

"I can't. It's too complicated, and too silly. It would sound so feeble in words, John. But feeling as you do about Rowena, you must understand at least some of it. Oh, I do so hope that you and she—"

"One hopes, always. And in the meantime one contrives, endures. Jenny, will you tell me one thing? This business with the Earl—is it an entirely one-sided affair? Or was there not a certain amount of two-way traffic?"

"Two-way traffic," she admitted. "But—I suppose you'd have to say it got diverted."

"By the same old immovable object?"

"To some extent. But it wasn't all the old woman's fault. I was a great deal to blame, being rather a fool in these matters."

"Well," said John, "I can imagine you a great many things, but a fool isn't one of them. I'm sorry you must go, Jenny. But you'll keep in close touch, won't you? We aren't barred, I hope?"

"Oh, John, of course not! And later, maybe, when I've come to my senses again, I'll come and see you. It's only that, just now, the place is unbearable. I have to go."

It wasn't fair, all the same, to leave quite at once. She had an obligation to Edward Channing and to the Print Room.

"I'm very sorry you should feel you have to go," Edward told her. "For Clare's sake as well as my own. Quite where we shall find a replacement for you I don't know—but you mustn't worry about it. If you could hang on a week longer I daresay we shall come up with something. What are your plans? You'll be living at home, I suppose?"

"I should think so, unless a job somewhere miraculously presents itself. But it didn't before, so I don't see why it should do so now."

The week of waiting was miserable. She could somehow no longer feel that she was one of the family at Morleys; she rode with them still, and swam and walked, but inside herself she felt like a stranger. Clare and John had made some kind of explanation to their parents, though she was not sure quite how much of the truth had been in it; the Morleys were regretful and kind, but in a vague sort of way, as though her affairs hardly impinged on their own. She was, in fact, alone. She had made her decision, and it had removed her from them already.

It did not help that every day she had to pass the

Hoppner portrait in the Long Gallery. She began to feel that perhaps what she had fallen in love with was no more than this thing of paint and canvas, as if it and the Earl were one, and she in some kind of curious dream caught by the hard glitter of painted grey eyes. "I am without conscience," they said to her. "I have all the charm in the world, and no heart—and you have no defence against either my charm or my heartlessness."

Of course it wasn't really so. But much of this man's blood ran in Charles Langton's veins; he had inherited the pride and the ruthlessness, and all of the charm. And it was true that she had no defence against him. If she could have defended herself any other way, then it would have been unnecessary for her to run away.

At the end of the week she packed and went home. Clare and John took her to the station and waved the train out with strained, bright smiles. Part of her own misery was the knowledge that she had caused them concern, had let them down, and as the train drew out of the station she leaned back in her seat by the window and closed her eyes against scalding tears. When she opened them again, it was to see Langton Castle set like a crown upon its distant hill, white against a blue sky, and the trees all green beneath it.

Such splendour could never have been hers. How could she for one minute have believed it? Such things happened only in fairy tales—and she was not Cinderella, she had left no glass slipper behind to bring him to her side. Only a sheaf of reasonably competent drawings—and they had been very properly paid for.

One day she would stop wanting Charles Langton. Even the strongest fires must die for lack of fuel, she knew that. But she would never quite forget him, nor any of this strange Cinderella summer, and perhaps never again would she love with such fierce intensity as she loved him now.

Her mother was wise enough not to ask too many questions, but could not resist a certain element of told-you-so in her reaction to Jenny's story.

"There was a man," Jenny explained that evening, as they sat over supper in the quiet little kitchen. The house seemed oppressively small. In the tiny garden, sun gilded the topmost leaves of the apple tree. "I found that I was in danger of making a fool of myself over him," she elaborated briefly. "So I thought I'd better come home."

"Poor old Jenny! But I did have my doubts. It's not easy to go from one level to another, is it? What was the problem—wasn't he available, or just not interested?"

"Not available. And not all that honourable, either. In fact, he was dangerous."

"Oh dear! People in that social bracket simply don't have the same ideas of propriety as ourselves, do they? Money anaesthetises the moral sense, somehow. I've never understood why it should, but it obviously does. You're really better off away from them, darling, however pleasant the life may have been."

"It was very pleasant. I learned to ride."

"Well, you don't have to give that up. There are stables in Benchley—"

"Oh, it wouldn't be the same! I'd rather never ride again than have to take out some miserable riding school hack!"

"Then perhaps it's as well you are back home," said her mother tartly. "Otherwise you'd soon have become too spoiled ever to be liveable with again."

Jenny felt ashamed. Maybe life with the Morleys hadn't been entirely good for her. She had very soon learned from them to want only the best, and that was arrogant, as well as being extremely unpractical.

"I'm sorry," she said. "I didn't mean to be so uppity. I have been spoiled, and you're quite right—being used to having the best of everything does make one selfish. Very charming, but selfish."

Determinedly she set about trying to forget them. For a time she wanted no contact even with the Morleys. They weren't corrupted by wealth, of course; even in her most bitter moments she couldn't believe that. But they were too much coloured by the dream that was over; they belonged to Langton and to a way of life that she must put behind her.

She tried to get back into some ordinary pattern of living. It wasn't easy; she had not enough to occupy her, finding housework dull, and walks in the village or bus rides into Oxford aimless. She could drum up no enthusiasm for the humdrum chores of everyday. Again she wrote to galleries, and followed up every chance advertisement that seemed to offer some hope of a job suited to her talents and qualifications. But as before, she seemed always to be either too well qualified or too little experienced. And she did not feel, now, that she dared offer her time at Langton as evidence of valid experience. She couldn't exactly ask for a reference, after the way she had behaved.

One evening Mrs. Rowland brought home a friend, the art teacher from the school where she worked.

"Ned has ideas about a job for you," she told Jenny. "I thought he'd better come and explain it for himself."

Ned was a large man, middle aged but energetic, with long black hair that flopped about his head and horn-rimmed glasses usually held together at some vital spot by sticking plaster. His hands were permanently paint-stained. Jenny liked him.

"Rotten for you being out of work so long, Jen," he commiserated, crashing down into an armchair and spreading his long legs over most of the floor. "We can't let it go on, can we? When your ma told me, I had a little ring round as many of my friends as I could think of who might be able to help. Now, there's this chap in London who runs a gallery. Quite high class, just off Knightsbridge, well in the picture-buying-as-an-investment belt. Now, all he wants at the moment is a reasonably knowledgeable receptionist. Hardly making use of your full abilities, as I told him, but it would be a foot in the door, and there's always the chance that something more interesting would turn up eventually. He's willing to have a look at you, anyway. What do you say?"

It was hard to say anything with gratitude making such a huge lump in her throat, but she managed to stammer out thanks of a kind. He waved a large, grubby hand.

"Think nothing of it. I'm only too glad to have been able to do something. I can't remember exactly what it was like to be young, but I do remember the misery of being hard up and fed up, with nothing to look forward to. Doesn't do any good to anyone. Talent gets lost in the scrabble for existence. And we can't have that happening to you."

But it so easily could have done, Jenny thought. And here was the difference between people of the Langtons' kind and people who had known real hardship. The Earl might have offered patronage, because that came easily to him; he bought pictures, and the artist incidentally benefited. But Ned had made a real effort, both in thought and the expenditure of time, and had found a practical solution to her problem. And he wanted no reward for it. His motive had been entirely altruistic. Whereas she could not ever imagine a Langton buying a worthless picture just because the artist was in need.

It was the kind of job seldom advertised, because there were so many people always ready to step into such a vacancy. Most of them were already connected with the art world in one way or another, either through wealth or through influential friends—as, she supposed, she must now consider herself to have been, though it was hard to think of Ned as wielding great influence in the world of picture dealing. She went up to London to be interviewed on a perfect summer's day, with London all clean and fresh after a night's rain, the parks green, the sky a limpid blue beyond buildings of white and grey. The gallery was close by Harrods. She could imagine the sort of well-heeled people who shopped there calling in at the gallery afterwards and carrying off a Renoir or so slipped into their Harrods' bags. The pavement outside seemed designed to be crossed by fur-coated ladies making for the air-conditioned sanctuary of the Rolls.

The gallery was owned and run by Nicholas Behr. Daddy Behr, Ned had called him, and Jenny saw why. He was a very large man, broad-shouldered and shambling, with a short-sighted, peering kind of walk. But there was nothing short-sighted about the exceedingly bright eyes that surveyed her from beneath a shaggy mop of wiry grey hair.

"So you are the young lady so well spoken of by my old friend," he said, his accent thickly European. They were sitting in an office at the back of the gallery, a room of quiet, untidy but unmistakably well-bred elegance, with dull navy blue walls against which hung a Sickert and a Crome, and a quite lovely little Constable. Nicholas Behr's tastes were evidently traditional and impeccable.

"It was very good of Ned to take this trouble over me," she said, remembering not to perch on the edge of her chair and to keep her nervous hands still. Her mother had been full of good advice.

"You realise of course that the job has very little to do with art," Behr was saying. "More to do with money. You have to know what's in the gallery and on the market, and to be able to talk intelligently about both. I would want you to go through the catalogues of sales and mark them for me, which means that you must know your clients also. How are you with people? You look as though you might be able to deal with them all right." He sounded a trifle dubious, she thought. Hastily she reassured him.

"I've spent some time at Langton Castle, in the Print Room there, showing things to visitors and so on. Some of them were very knowledgeable."

"Mph! Ned mentioned you'd been moving in exalted circles. Some good things hanging on those fake mediaeval walls, eh? The Reynolds, and the Hoppner—!"

"Oh yes," she said palely. "The Hoppner."

"An eye for beauty, that family. Always had. I'd place it one of the best collections in England. But there, my girl, you didn't come to talk about other collections. Come and see mine. It changes, but I can promise you that we are never without something pretty good."

They went slowly along the walls of the L-shaped gallery. Here and there Nicholas Behr would stop to enthuse over a particular canvas, and there were questions too, some of them very sharp. Before they were two thirds of the way round Jenny felt that she had been thoroughly examined on her knowledge of the history of art and on the many different schools, techniques and styles of painting. Occasionally he wanted an opinion.

"I think here, you know, he was searching for a way to express the difference in tone without having to alter the emphasis. What do you think?"

She found that she did not mind being asked. The subject interested her, she knew what she was talking about, and so his questioning held no fears for her. Evidently Behr was satisfied. When they had made their tour of the gallery he took her back into the office and called a beautifully tailored young man who had been drifting vaguely about the place and asked him to provide sherry.

"We celebrate—I have found your successor, Henry," he said—not, Jenny thought, without a degree of waspish satisfaction. "You need feel obliged no longer."

"Glory be!" declared Henry, and wafted away to find the sherry. Behr watched him go.

"Ah well," he said. "We all have our momentary lapses of judgement. But you, dear lady, are not going to be another of them. I feel we shall get on well together. You have sense in that pretty head—and I ssupect you of possessing good manners, which alas one can no longer take for granted even in the most learned of persons. So, all in all, I think I would like you to work for me. Yes, I think I would like that very much. Assuming, of course, that you still want to."

"Oh, more than ever," she said, and meant it. The gallery had a solid kind of tranquillity; she could imagine being very happy working there, and she liked Daddy Behr.

"So," he said, nodding with satisfaction. "When can you start? Henry, as you see, wants nothing more than to leave me so that he can go and run a little shop with his dearest friend in Sloane Street—and I want nothing more than for that to be possible. Therefore I would be glad of your presence at the earliest moment you can make it."

"Well—" Doubt cast a sudden shadow. "I haven't got anywhere to live. And it's not easy to find somewhere, is it? I mean, accommodation in London—"

"Need be no problem." He beamed. "I have a daughter, and she has many friends. They are always moving in and out of flats. I am sure somewhere among them we can fit you in. Now—I suggest this. When you have finished your little drink, you will go and shop, or window-shop, or whatever it is women do that takes so long in London. Come back at about four. I will then have solved your little problem."

"Really?" She looked at him in awe. "I shall begin to think you a magician. Not an angel—I'm sure you aren't that. But definitely a magician."

He chuckled, hugely delighted.

"Of course!" he said. "Magic is the easiest way to get what you want. I have always practised it. And I am so glad that you perceive that I am not an angel. It's a sound basis for friendship; we will drink to it."

Henry had returned with the sherry, and they

proceeded to drink to friendship, to each other, and even to the prosperity of Henry's best friend's little shoop in Sloane Street. Then Jenny took her leave.

"Come back at four," Daddy Behr reminded her as he showed her out of the gallery. "I shall have found you a *pied-a-terre*, and we will then discuss business. Don't worry. If I find you a home, I will see that you can afford to live in it."

The thought was consoling. She went out into the street feeling quite unreal, because suddenly, magically, things were going to be all right. She would have work to take her mind off Charles Langton and to restore her self-respect; she would have a foot in the door of the art world, and some kind of a home of her own in London. It was a little hard to believe, having all happened in the space of an hour or so.

She wandered along past Harrods' seductive windows, into Knightsbridge and thence into Hyde Park. Across the park it was not far to Oxford Street. And she had some money to spend. There was no longer any pressing need to hoard what she had earned at Langton; she could get rid of it all in the most satisfactory way. And somehow she did want to be rid of it.

She reached Marble Arch, and plunged with determination into the nearest large store, there to spend the Earl of Langton's patronage and so make herself free of him for ever.

Ten

When she returned to the gallery at four o'clock, Jenny was much encumbered by parcels and most of the Langton money had gone.

Daddy Behr was waiting for her with the benevolent air of a man well satisfied with himself. "Well, my young lady," he greeted her, "come and sit down and hear what I have to say. Put your shopping here, look. It was an enjoyable afternoon?"

"Very," she said with conviction, bestowing her parcels and bags in the curtained cloakroom alcove he had indicated. "I spent far too much, and feel thoroughly pleased with myself." She sat opposite him across the big desk and composed herself to hear what he should say. It must be good news, she was sure of it from his air of benign self-congratulation. Her heart was beating faster than it should, and she sat tensed almost as if at any moment she might have to leap up and run.

"Now then," he began, "I rang my daughter, and learned that a friend of hers, whom I know personally and can vouch for, has recently taken the lease of a house not so very far from here, in Blisham

Square. It is the kind of house that is split into one room flats. Several of her friends have taken sub-leases on these, but one remains vacant. I have bespoken it for you—but of course on condition that you like it when you have seen it. Would this arrangement be agreeable to you?"

"It sounds utterly perfect," said Jenny in a voice that shook slightly. "When could I see it?"

"Now, provided that you are able to take a late enough train home."

"Oh, it doesn't matter what time—"

"Splendid. Then I shall ask Henry to find you a taxi. It will take you there, wait for you and bring you back, so that we can finalise our business. You had better leave your parcels. Henry!" He clapped his hands, and the languid Henry materialised. "A taxi for Miss Rowland," Daddy Behr demanded.

Within a very few moments Jenny was in the taxi and on her way to Blisham Square. Number eighteen proved to be a typical tall, stuccoed house with a heavy portico and a great many large windows, in a terrace of identical dwellings, looking upon a central garden full of shrubs enclosed by iron railings. The edge of the pavement was lined with parked cars.

She had with her a note from Daddy Behr. Clutching it in her hand, she stood under the heavy canopy of the porch and rang the bell, while the taxi went grumbling off to circle the block until she should be ready to return.

The door was opened by a tall, thin girl dressed in jeans and a painty smock.

"Hello. Are you Jenny Rowland? Come in—and do please excuse the mess, but we've only just got going with redecoration."

The lofty hall was a jungle of step-ladders, dust sheets and cans of paint, and there was the smell of fresh paint everywhere. Jenny rather liked it. There seemed to be a great deal of white in the colour scheme, which was as well, because the hall was massively gloomy.

"I'm Leah, Tanya Behr's friend," the girl explained, threading her way through the chaos and starting up the stairs. "Come on, and I'll show you the flat. It's at the very top, I'm afraid, but it has a super light, and being at the top, converted from attics, it's quite big. Daddy Behr tells me you're an artist."

"Well—I suppose so. I'm not quite sure how one qualifies."

"By doing it, I should think—painting and drawing, I mean. You don't have to make a living at it. Lots of the best hardly ever sell a thing."

"That's conforting," said Jenny. They were on the second flight, and already she began to be conscious of shaky knees. "How far to the top?"

"Another two flights. Do you mind?"

"I daresay I shall become hardened. I'm not in training just at the moment."

The last flight was the most taxing. It was narrow and uncarpeted, and she felt afraid of stumbling against the steep risers of the steps. But at the top there was a white-painted corridor with two doors, and one of these opened into a marvellous long attic room with a sloping roof half of glass, coming down to within six feet of the floor before the far wall met it. There was a French door which opened onto a tiny balcony. Beyond this rose a mountain range of blue slate rooftops punctuated by outcrops of chimney stacks, and the sun shone slanting between them.

There was a bare minimum of furniture; a divan bed, a chest of drawers, a table and four chairs.

"It's let furnished, because that protects me, tenancy laws being what they are," explained Leah. "But of course you import what you like, and do anything to it, within reason—I mean, I'd rather you didn't actually knock down walls, but barring that anything goes."

"Oh, it's perfect!" Jenny breathed. "I'd no idea—I thought an ordinary bed-sit or something, but this—"

"There's a kitchen at the end, and a bathroom—both minute, but reasonably adequate, I think."

They were more than adequate; they seemed to Jenny quite unbelievably luxurious. The kitchen had a window looking out over the rooftops, and contained an electric cooker, steel sink, fridge and several capacious white cupboards. The bathroom was mink-coloured and tiny. She could imagine living there for ever in perfect comfort, and if total happiness was dependent on Charles Langton, then at least she could be reasonably contented here without him.

The rent seemed a great deal, but she was not yet used to London prices, and Daddy Behr had promised her that she would be able to afford it. Recklessly she settled with Leah that she would move in some time the following week. Then she went to wait for her taxi, and was soon back at the gallery and making her final arrangements with Daddy Behr. Exactly one week later, on a Thursday, she moved into the flat in Blisham Square.

She had until the following Monday to settle in and get used to living there. Mrs. Rowland, as if released from bondage, at once put their house on the market and moved into an Oxford flat—so promptly, indeed, that Jenny felt a pang of remorse, suspecting that it was only her own need of a home that had held her mother back all this time. It was as if an era had ended—childhood, perhaps, and the expectation of security it induced. Jenny was alone, really alone, for the first time, an independent unit, self-supporting. She felt elated, and at the same time just a little afraid.

The most irritating thing to get used to was the constant traffic noise of London. It was always there, even through the night, a roaring sound like surf breaking on shingle. She had forgotten how restless London was—and how exhilarating. Her first weekend was spent in stocking up the kitchen, making curtains, arranging the books and pictures and small items of furniture she had brought from home. On the Sunday she explored her immediate neighbourhood. At one point, passing a telephone box, she was moved by a sudden impulse to discover, if she could, the Langtons' town address. Of course, they were probably ex-directory, it was the

fashionable thing these days. All the same she
hauled out the heavy directory and began to leaf
through its torn, scribbled and dirty pages, aching
with a ridiculous access of nerves, almost as
though she were actually going to see him. And
despite every expectation to the contrary his name
was there, and his address—one square away from
that in which she had come to live.

It was the most cruel coincidence. She had walked
through Milton Square several times already, not
knowing, and she wished that she did not know
now. Fool, to have tried to find him—fool to have
tempted fate. She had thought herself free of him,
only to discover that she had run, figuratively if not
literally, straight into his arms again.

Of course, there was no reason why they should
ever meet. Milton Square was another social bracket entirely from that in which Jenny lived; the cars
parked along its pavements were custom built by
Bentley and Mercedes. The Harrods belt began
there. She had no need ever to walk that way, and
she could not imagine that the Langtons, any of
them, would ever find it necessary to enter Blisham
Square. Yet even as she told herself this her feet had
begun to carry her in the direction of Milton Square,
and she knew that she would not be able to
suppress her knowledge that sometimes, at least,
he would be as close to her as ever he had been
at Langton.

The houses in Milton Square were elegant and
quiet, their stuccoed fronts painted in pastel
shades, flowering window boxes and graceful

wrought iron area railings all proclaiming a solid prosperity. Even the pavements seemed particularly clean. At intervals they were shaded by leafy plane trees, and here and there the pale terraces were broken by archways leading to cobbled mews. Jenny almost expected to hear the clatter of horseshoes and the trundle of carriage wheels.

The Langton house was very much like all the rest. She walked by it rapidly with her head down, stricken by a sudden terror lest she should be seen and recognised. But it was most likely that they had gone back to Tathwell by now. The house no doubt stood empty, waiting until they might briefly want it again—perhaps when autumn came and there were things to do in London once more. And maybe by then it would no longer matter to her where Charles Langton lived when he was in town.

But she had broken through her defence against him. Now, whenever she sat alone in her flat among the rooftops she would be aware of the possibility of his being near. She would picture that house and imagine him there, the pavements would be haunted by the chance of meeting him. Bitterly she regretted her inability to leave well alone. She had done with him; there was no reason why she should have needed or wanted to know where he lived when he was in London. She had managed to cut herself off from everything else that had to do with Langton; why could she not have denied herself that knowledge too?

It was a relief to be able to start work in the Behr gallery. She liked Daddy Behr, and not just because he had been instrumental in organising her new life. He made a perfect father figure, while possessing also a large, cosmopolitan kind of glamour which made her feel somehow more sophisticated herself, more knowledgeable and worldly than really she was. He paid her the subtlest of all compliments in assuming her to be capable of understanding anything he might say to her or require of her; he treated her as a child, a woman and an equal, and all of them at once. She wasn't used to this kind of flattery; she basked in it, soaked it up, and became therefore rapidly more and more like the image of herself that he held constantly before her. By the end of that summer she had grown up a great deal.

The work was always interesting. Best of all she liked browsing among catalogues, marking in them items for Daddy Behr's attention. Then sometimes there was the thrill of accompanying him to sales. She increasingly enjoyed meeting the people who congregated there, and who came from time to time into the gallery. At first it had been difficult; she was conscious always of their wealth and poise contrasted with her own lack of confidence. But little by little her self-assurance grew and her awe of them diminished, until she found that she took a positive delight in practising her charm upon them, making herself agreeable to them—putting into effect, indeed, the same process of flattery she had learned at first hand from Daddy Behr himself. It was new to her, this realisation that she could manipulate people by the conscious exercise of charm. And yet if she had not been so blind and so young she ought to have learned it at Langton, for there they were all masters of the art. Charm was their defence and their justification; it allowed them to use people without ever feeling the least guilt, since their victims were so willing to be used, almost as though to be exploited with such charm were a privilege granted only to the chosen few.

She must be growing hard and old, Jenny thought, to see the mechanics of it with such clarity. And if she were hardened to such an extent, there was very little the Langtons could do to hurt her now. All the same she avoided Milton Square, and resolutely blocked out of her mind all thought of his possible nearness. It was exhausting sometimes, the effort of not thinking of him, and it left a kind of dead area in her consciousness, as though part of her mind were quite numb. But numbness was better than pain; at least it allowed the rest of her to live.

Summer declined into autumn. All the trees in London seemed dusty and tired, ready to give up their leaves. The grass in the parks was thin and brown, and Jenny felt that she had lived in London for ever. No longer a student scarcely out of college, nor a country girl come up to town, she had turned into a Londoner, a career woman, groomed and sleek and sure of herself. Surely by now she had begun to get over Charles Langton.

Hearts didn't break. She had learned that. They could feel as though they had broken, but gradually the aching dulled, the hurt and humiliation faded and became uninteresting. It was curious, though, that such a deadness followed. Despite every strenuous effort on Daddy Behr's part, she felt no flicker of attraction towards the succession of charming and undoubtedly highly eligible young men who began to find their way to the gallery. Occasionally she went out with one or other of them to the theatre, to Tramps or some similar dive, or to a concert. They were all delightful young men, though pressed out of moulds so similar that she sometimes had trouble in remembering which of them was which. But they roused no spark of feeling in her, save for a general appreciation of their company and a certain amused acknowledgement of the compliment they paid her by so assiduously trying. It was perhaps too soon. After such intense emotion as she had experienced during the Langton episode, there had to be a time of numbness. It was like recovering from a wound; the area of feeling was anaesthetised. In time, no doubt, her capacity for feeling would return—and with it the risk of being hurt again.

It was a dull, close sort of day, the sky over London piled high with purple clouds. No doubt the weather would break soon. Rain would come as a relief; the air had been sultry now for days, as if the lingering heat of summer had thickened into something almost solid. Inside the gallery all the lights were on. Jenny sat in the office, a pile of catalogues in front of her, a red marker in her hand. There had been few visitors; it wasn't the kind of day for buying pictures, somehow, the air was too oppressive, and people who could be out of town had gone, away from the sticky, depressing heat.

She heard the gallery door open, but did not stir, knowing that Daddy Behr was about somewhere; he had spent much of the day debating as to the exact spot in which to display a Corot that had just come into his hands, and was probably now rapt in contemplation of the picture—worrying, maybe, whether just a few inches to the left or to the right might not make all the difference between complete perfection and disaster. With a small part of her attention she listened to make quite sure that he was there and that the gallery was not left unattended.

She heard him speak, and without catching his words registered the fact that it was no casual visitor, but someone deemed worthy of the very smoothest Behr-brand treatment. Then the visitor spoke.

Jenny sat rigid in her chair. In her head the blood began to roar, and everything around her seemed to fade into a dim, clammy twilight. She gripped the edge of the table and bit her tongue to prevent herself from making a sound.

It was Charles Langton. His quiet, diffident voice seemed to leap the gulf of months and brought her at once into his presence; she saw, as if he were close enough to touch, the mocking grey eyes, the little one-sided smile, the thick fair hair. His image suffocated her; she jerked to her feet in panic and fled like a terrified animal to the furthest corner of the office, cowering there, ready to dive through the curtain into the cloakroom if there should be the least danger of their coming near her.

Through the pounding noise in her head she caught little gusts of speech.

". . . rather special," Charles was saying. "The wedding isn't until the end of October, so there's time . . ."

"The Corot is quite the best thing I have in at the moment. But perhaps—?"

"If there were anything English?"

"Well—a Constable? But not the most distinguished, as you see. However, I could look through the list of what is coming on the market, if you give me a moment. My assistant—"

Jenny heard him lumbering towards the office. Tingling with alarm she slipped behind the curtain, and listened as he rummaged about the desk, muttering to himself in a disgruntled manner. Presently he returned into the gallery where Charles Langton waited. There was a protracted murmuring in which Jenny could distinguish nothing comprehensible. But it hardly mattered. She had heard enough. By the kind of irony with which such things commonly fall out, the Earl had come to this gallery in search of a wedding gift for his future countess. Amelia, no doubt, though it scarcely mattered. It wasn't herself, and that was all she cared about. She hadn't believed that it could still hurt so much.

She wanted to put her head over the cloakroom basin and be sick. Every inch of her was cold, and her legs would hardly hold her up; she trembled, feeling the old wound ripped open, raw and agonising as it had always been under the barriers of carefully built scar tissue. Hearing his voice was enough. She wanted him as desperately as she had ever done, and there would be no other man in the world she would ever want so much. All that time had done for her was to allow her the temporary balm of self-deception.

She was hardly conscious of the gallery door's opening and closing at last. Weakly she leaned against the wall behind the curtain, and when Daddy Behr came calling her she could not for a moment bring herself to face him.

"You missed an interesting and valuable client!" he was grumbling. "And what is more, you could have been useful, knowing the catalogues better than I do. What have you been up to, girl?"

She emerged from the curtained alcove, and one look at her face was enough to silence him. He took her by the shoulders, pushed her into a chair and poured a large brandy.

"Drink!" he commanded. Trembling, she did so, and shuddered at the taste. But gradually a fiery warmth spread from where the brandy had gone and she began to feel a little better.

"Silly of me," she said shakily. "I felt a bit faint. I'm sorry."

"Hmph!" He regarded her fiercely from beneath the bushy brows. "And why, I ask myself, do healthy modern young ladies have these sudden fits of the vapours? And then I remember that you have

worked for some time for Lord Langton. Could it be
that you are reluctant to meet him? Why, I wonder?"

"I—didn't want to meet him," she murmured, her
voice hardly audible.

"Why not? Did you remove something of value
from his collection, maybe?"

"No! Oh no." Despite herself she laughed, though
tears were perilously near. "It really wasn't anything
like that."

"The man himself then. Aha!" Daddy Behr nodded his huge, sagacious head, intelligence gleaming
in his eyes. "He is a most personable young man, is
he not? And you—I will not believe you have no
heart, though you are so unkind to my lovely young
men I find for you. It is Lord Langton, all the time,
who makes you blind to others."

"But I thought I was getting over it!" she protested childishly. "I didn't know he could still
devastate me. I thought I was cured of him."

"It's hard to cure the heart of love." He peered at
her from under the shaggy brows. "And does he not
return all this emotion? Is he after all a blind man?"

"He's an Earl. And the Langtons are proud."

"Ah!" Again he nodded. "Tell me," he invited her.
"You can trust me. I will understand, and it will help
you to tell someone."

Perhaps he was right, she thought. And certainly,
of all the people she knew, he was the most likely to
understand. Haltingly, and somewhat sketchily, she
began to tell him what had happened at Langton,
and about the havoc it had wrought in her life.

Eleven

True to his word, Daddy Behr was a sympathetic and understanding listener.

"It's too bad!" he declared when she had finished her dismal little story. "I will not allow such things! This Countess—I know a little about her, and she is a hard woman, very hard—very much the *Grande Dame*, no? Somehow I feel it would be a good thing for the world at large if for once she were to be opposed."

"But there's nothing to be done. He'll marry Amelia, and then—"

"Maybe. She has money, of course, and the breeding of a racehorse. But what does a man want with a horse in bed? I would have thought the Earl to have a little more red blood in him."

"She's very beautiful," said Jenny with an effort. "And she's at home in his kind of world."

"Only because she has lived in it. One can become accustomed to anything." Daddy Behr spoke absently and in a depressed tone, as if he were contemplating the situation and finding it both distasteful and inescapable.

"Then I can get used to the fact that I can't ever have him," pointed out Jenny. "I thought I was beginning to do so—I quite thought I'd swallowed the notion that love stories don't always have a happy ending. But—hearing his voice again when I wasn't expecting it—I panicked. I couldn't have faced him. One day I shall, though. You'll see."

"Without a doubt, if you are to remain here, one day you will have to meet him. He is a valuable client." Behr shrugged. "We shall see. But in the meantime, child, life must go on—a lesson you have learned already. So let us for the moment forget your troubles and look at what you have found me in your search through these lists. The Romney, now. It interests the Earl. I shall make arrangements to look at it for myself."

They were back to the commonplace business of the day. It was time to close the gallery, time for Jenny to clear her desk and go home. She went out into the streets feeling curiously unreal. It was a stifling, still evening, with brooding clouds threatening a storm, and air hot and electric dry as the inside of an oven. All London seemed subdued, tense and depressed as Jenny herself felt. Walking along the Brompton Road, she found herself mentally picturing Langton, where autumn would not be a matter of shrivelling and dying as it was here, but rich with flame softened by mists, ripeness not quite tumbled into decay. If only the place had not been so beautiful! Often and often in a morning, before she had quite woken up, she imagined herself there again. Birds singing in the Kensington treetops would sound for that few moments like the songbirds at Langton, and until she opened her eyes on her attic room it was easy to believe herself in bed at Morleys with a morning's ride before her and an afternoon in the hushed, papery-smelling Print Room.

Clare and her family were a recurrent source of guilt and regret. She had promised to keep in touch with them, but the effort of doing so had threatened so much pain that she had found it simpler to include them in her wholesale rejection of Langton. So they had no address for her now. She had asked her mother to forward nothing, even supposing a letter should be sent on from the old house. It was a mean kind of cowardice and she was ashamed of it, but she could not bring herself to renew contact with them yet, even so remotely as by letter. It was best all forgotten—or so she told herself.

She felt, all the same, bitterly lonely. Letting herself into the silent attic flat that night, and living through the days that followed, she found that despite her every effort the people at Langton occupied more and more of her mind. It was as if the shock of encountering Charles again—even though she had only heard his voice—had thrown open in her head a door which she no longer had the power to shut. The Morleys and Edward Channing suddenly seemed more real to her than the people she met every day. Their voices ran on in her head, little fragments of conversation she would find herself holding with them, seeking their opinion as if they were actually present with her all the time.

And more than all the others she heard Charles Langton speaking to her, as he had done that day at Tathwell.

"It's a dangerous game," he had said. "I wouldn't play it if I were you—not unless you're prepared to lose."

She hadn't been prepared, of course. One never was. The thought of losing had no meaning for her then, because love had dazzled her; the longing she had felt for him had seemed stronger than anything. She hadn't understood him at all. But he had understood the precarious unreality of their situation. No doubt he had envisaged his mother's reaction, too. Jenny could hear her voice as clearly as all the rest. "A little diversion, no more; they happen from time to time . . ." Detached, more matter-of-fact than malicious; they had considered her much as they might have conferred over the inadequacies of a new parlour maid or the unsatisfactoriness of some local tradesman. She was still shaken by fury when she thought of it—the fury of helplessness and humiliation. Time had repaired nothing. She was as much involved with them all as if she had never left the place; perhaps even more so. For in running away she had stopped the clock for ever at that moment. Apart from Langton she could not resolve anything, there could be no development, but only the same weary stalemate, the bitterness and sense of loss.

She watched the papers for news of the impending wedding. It was as well to know the worst. At least then the stubborn spark of hope would be finally quenched; it would be progress of a kind. Opening *The Times* in the gallery each day was a self-inflicted torture, and even to herself she could not pretend that she skimmed its pages for anything that might be useful to Daddy Behr. But there was no report of the wedding, no hint of its imminence, and so despite everything hope still flickered, though she hated herself for hoping or even caring.

Daddy Behr had embarked on a determined campaign to take her out of herself. He chivvied her and jollied her, and worked her at such a pace that she had little leisure for brooding. Sometimes he took her with him to view before a sale, or actually to the auction itself, so that she began to have some idea of that side of the picture business—a curious mixture of erudite scholarship, reverence for art and hard financial maneuvering, it was really a businessman's world. The sums of money changing hands were so large as to seem unreal—at least to Jenny they were unreal; she would never have so much money in her life as some of these squares of paint-covered canvas could command. It seemed senseless, mad, to pay so much for anything made by a man. It wasn't even as if the artist were going to benefit; in almost every case the artist was long ago dead and past caring.

Not always, though. Daddy Behr had a certain rather cautious interest in some modern painters.

"One must be very discriminating," he maintained. "Judgement is largely retrospective—we can only place a talent by seeing it in the context of its age, and we cannot get far enough away from our own age to see it clearly. So contemporary work is hard to judge unless the talent should be so startling as to transcend every such consideration."

Dan Barnaby was one such exception to the rule. Daddy Behr was always ready to acquire any canvas he might care to put on the market, and had even been known to complain that the man didn't sell enough.

"Here is an artist who cannot put brush to canvas without saying something that matters, and yet left to himself he would be quite content to paint only for his own amusement. He could be rich, fêted, adored—and he chooses obscurity. I tell you, little girl, this is a crazy, cruel world! Who'd be a poor struggling picture dealer, trying to make a living out of the whims of such people?"

It seemed, however, that this year Barnaby had been persuaded into an effort enough to fill a London exhibition.

"You will come with me to the private view," Jenny was told. "It's an important occasion and good for your education. I understand that there are portraits."

"Is that unusual?"

"For this man. He is selective about whom he paints. Sometimes they are rich—but always interesting."

Jenny tried to remember whether she had ever seen any portrait by Dan Barnaby. She knew his name; one could not be interested in pictures and not know it. There was a canvas of his in the Tate, she recalled—an abstract, tingling with colour and vitality. She could believe that a portrait by such a painter would be worth seeing. Besides, a private view was something novel; so far all the collections she had seen had been by painters now unable to put a price on their own work. It would be instructive to discover what Dan Barnaby or his agent expected people to pay for his pictures, and what sort of people were anxious to buy them.

It was an evening occasion at a large gallery off Bond Street. Jenny had time to go home from work to bathe and change before Daddy Behr's car called for her. She dressed with especial care and formality in a long-skirted, severe silk suit the colour of dark flame. She didn't want to let Daddy Behr down; no doubt the place would be full of elegant, expensive women of the kind who sat mink-clad at picture sales and bid enormous sums of money as though they were playing Monopoly. In appearance, if not in purchasing power, Jenny felt bound to hold her own. Apart from any other consideration, it was good for business.

Daddy Behr appreciated the gesture.

"Very *chic*, very good!" he declared, examining her from top to toe as if she might be a Reubens or a Manet newly come into the gallery. "With any luck they will take you for my mistress. My credit at once will be raised."

The rooms off Bond Street were already moderately crowded when they arrived. There was a great deal of fur and glitter, a heavy mingling of perfume in the air, and conversation that went on in several languages. Jenny was presented with a glass of sherry and a catalogue, and then Daddy Behr guided her into the first room, muttering: "We look first, talk later. I am a businessman."

Almost at once they encountered Dan Barnaby himself. It surprised Jenny to find that he was still a young man; somehow she had imagined that an artist of his stature, though still technically living, must be very near the point of extinction. On the contrary, Barnaby was in his early thirties, and possessed a kind of wistful charm which made him seem younger still.

"So, Daddy Behr," he greeted the dealer. "Here I am with a gallery full enough to please even you— and lots of them big ones. Now complain that I don't exhibit or sell enough to keep the wolf from your door."

"Hmph!" Daddy Behr peered around him at the canvases hanging against the pale, expensive walls. "About time, too. There's such a thing as duty, my boy. This is my new assistant, Jenny Rowland. One day I would like to see a decent portrait of her."

The painter's extraordinarily clear blue eyes rested thoughtfully upon Jenny.

"Rowland," he said. "That's a name I've come across recently. Now where? Jenny Rowland. . . ."

She thought it somehow unlikely.

"Perhaps there's another one somewhere," she suggested. "I make no claim to uniqueness."

A smile flashed at her. "Oh, but I'm sure you're quite unique—the name cropped up, but I can't remember where."

Daddy Behr was already fidgeting, rumbling uneasily, rather like a dormant but unsettled volcano.

"Pictures," he said. "I came to look at them. I leave you to your interesting speculations." And he stumped over to the paintings on the nearer wall and began to examine them with ferocious concentration.

"I like your boss," Dan Barnaby said to Jenny, amusement dancing in his eyes. "How do you get on with him?"

"I adore him. He's one of the kindest people I've ever met—really, I owe so much to him."

"So do a great many people, I suspect. Unusual to be able to say that of a hard-headed businessman. At the moment, however, he seems to have abandoned you. May I show you some of the better stuff?"

"Well thank you, but—"

"My pleasure."

So Jenny was taken on a tour of the pictures by their painter, and found the experience illuminating and interesting.

"It's obvious that you're something of a painter yourself," he said at one point, when she had asked him a particularly technical question as to his method of mixing paint. "Perhaps that's why I've heard your name before?"

"Oh, I've never got to the point where people

would talk about me as a painter. I'm really an art historian. But I do draw and paint a little, for my own satisfaction."

It seemed somehow absurd to consider herself an artist in the presence of such a radiant talent as this man had. She was bemused and dazzled by the evidence of his virtuosity which hung all around her. There was such conviction, such absolute rightness about everything he did, abstracts, landscapes, design—and now they had come into the room where the portraits were hung, and Jenny knew before she had seen them that they would be magnificent. He was quite simply a very great painter, whereas she would never be more than a competent one.

"We put the portraits all together," he was saying, "since for once there were enough of them to fill a room. I'm notoriously mean with my portraiture. Painting the wealthy is the one certain way to become fashionable, and I refuse to be that."

The room was longer than it was wide, and the smaller portraits, studies of heads and so on had been arranged along the sides, a kind of anvenue leading the eye along to the single huge canvas on the end wall, which dominated them all. Jenny looked at it, and felt her stomach lurch sickeningly as if she had just stepped on ground that had failed beneath her. She struggled for self-possession, but felt the colour draining from her face.

It had been painted very much after the style of the great English portraitists of the eighteenth century, yet its strength and the luminous clarity of its colouring were unmistakably Barnaby's own. As for the subject, Jenny had no need to consult her catalogue. The Lady Rowena Langton had been set by the artist against the misty English landscape of Langton Park, with the castle on its hill in the background. She wore a long muslin dress, white with pale yellow sash, and carried a straw hat in her hand.

Slowly Jenny walked towards the picture, and came to stand in front of it as if hypnotised.

"That one's not for sale," Dan Barnaby said behind her. "But they were good enough to let me have it to show. I'm rather pleased with it."

"You caught her exactly. Pretty, but terribly English and just a little shy."

"Ah!" There was triumph in his voice. "That's where I heard of you. Of course, it was at Langton. Oh, but—"

"I was there for a time, helping with the summer tourist jamboree. But I didn't entirely care for—for certain aspects of it. So I left. No doubt they told you."

"Yes . . ." He was standing beside her, looking at her now with a kind of indecision. All about them was the subdued buzz of conversation, the rustle and shuffle of movement, as little groups of people came near and then retreated to a well-bred distance from the artist, pretending that they were anything but interested in his intense, murmured conversation with Nicholas Behr's girl. Jenny was scarcely aware of their presence. Suddenly she burned to know what he had been told about her at

Langton; she was desperate to know, yet pride would not let her admit it.

"Perhaps they're friends of yours," she said diffidently, and bit on her tongue to stop it from saying more.

"Only in the line of business. I thought they were more friends of yours—or that he was, anyway."

"Oh?" Her heart was throbbing hard enough to choke her. "Why?" she asked, her voice quavering despite her effort to control it.

"He seemed anxious to trace you. As a matter of fact he showed me some drawings you'd done—wondered if I might have come across you."

"Oh." She felt thoroughly bemused. She had expected to hear almost anything but that—a diatribe against her from the Countess, perhaps, or an account of her infatuation and subsequent flight made into an amusing anecdote. Not that the Earl wanted to find her. There was no reason in the world why he should ever want to set eyes on her again. He was going to marry Amelia.

"Did you not meet Lady Amelia?" she asked Dan Barnaby now, her voice harsh with sudden resentment that all this should be raked up yet again, like an unending persecution. "I'd have thought you more likely to be painting her portrait to hang in the Langton gallery after they're married."

"Lady Amelia? I don't remember her. But it's Rowena who's getting married, you know—to a chap from the estate, a vet or something. That's why they got me to paint her. It's the family tradition when a daughter marries."

"Rowena getting married! To John Morley? Is that the name?"

"That's the fellow. And his sister's marrying the Earl's secretary. I assure you, the air was clamorous with wedding bells, but none of them for the Earl— or not that I noticed."

"Oh dear—" Jenny felt suddenly weak, and very much as though she might disgrace herself by bursting into tears. "Oh dear," she said shakily. "The whole subject's a bit fraught—and it's a shock, to find—"

"I'm sorry." He put a hand under her arm and turned her away from the portrait, guiding her at a careful, steady pace down the long room. She could feel eyes upon them from every side despite an elaborate pretence at indifference on all the faces she could see; it was probably going to be the sensation of the evening. Nicholas Behr's girl going off with the artist in this notably interesting manner. She could have laughed at them all, only it wasn't safe to laugh because the tears were so very near.

"Really," she protested in an embarrassed mutter, "I'm all right. I mean, I'm not going to have hysterics or anything."

"Aren't you? But I can feel you shaking."

"I promise to shake quietly."

They came to a standstill in the outer room where the landscapes hung. All around them the crowd chattered and shifted, an indistinct blur, a forest of trailing skirts and white shirt fronts. Jenny wondered if she could be going to faint, the world about her seemed so unreal. But one thing she had to get clear in her head, one urgent question over-riding all the rest; it seemed to swim up at her out of the confusion of all he had said, and to nullify everything else.

"But you say he wanted to trace me? He asked you if you knew me? And he's not going to marry the Lady Amelia! I don't understand—I thought—"

His hand tightened on her arm.

"You could ask him," Dan Barnaby said.

He was looking beyond her towards the door. Jenny froze. The room seemed to have gone suddenly, unnaturally still, as if everyone in it were turned to stone. Even before she turned to look she knew what had happened—and knew, all in a moment, why Daddy Behr had wanted her with him this evening of all others.

The Earl of Langton and the Dowager Countess stood just inside the doorway. In the moment of stillness before they moved forward, before it became necessary for her to move or to speak, Jenny's impression of them was extraordinarily acute. The Dowager seemed shrunken and faded, an old woman suddenly, the china blue eyes filmed over with disappointment and discontent. And her son was a distinguished stranger. Contained, authoritative, strong—but a stranger; it was as if Jenny had never seen him before in her life.

Dan Barnaby propelled her forward. Left to herself she might have stayed still and perhaps have escaped notice; she did not know what she might have done. But it was too late now. Looking about him, Charles Langton met her eyes; she saw warm colour surge up beneath the fair, tanned skin, and all at once he was a stranger no more, he was the man she loved and wanted above everything in the world, and she moved towards him with all the inevitability of a creature gripped by fate.

"Charles." Her voice sounded strange in her own ears; it shook with the force of pent-in feeling. But all around them were people watching, listening; it wouldn't do to make any kind of a scene. And so, somehow, she held out her hand to him and said: "I didn't know you would be here. But I'm glad—"

"Hello, Jenny." His voice was low and shaken, and the hand that clasped hers gripped so hard that it hurt, yet still she could feel the tremor that ran through him. His grey eyes met hers steadily; but at the corner of his mouth a little pulse beat, and betrayed him.

"I hardly expected to see you here either," he said. "You seemed to have disappeared off the face of the earth."

"I came to London to work for Nicholas Behr." She made a desperate effort to control her voice, to make it conversational and light. A chance meeting between acquaintances who had been out of touch, that was the keynote; yet had it not been for the clasp of his hand still hard on hers she felt that she must have fallen to the ground, so devastating was the ache of longing, the raw need for him that flooded through and through her.

"We were worried about you," he said. "Clare and John and everyone. It was—unkind, not to let us know—"

"Things happened so quickly. And besides, I thought—oh, it seemed best."

It hurt her to look at him. His hair was so fair and thick, and the grey eyes with their fringe of thick, fair lashes turned her heart over and over. A fierce, despairing kind of anger shook her at the thought that she had been so nearly free, so nearly cured of loving him. No doubt Daddy Behr had imagined it a good deed to throw her in Charles Langton's way, but really it was cruel of him. No good could come of reopening old wounds. The situation that had made them had not changed.

"I had to live, after all," she said roughly. "And Daddy Behr gave me a job."

"You had a job at Langton."

"But it wasn't really my kind of world, was it?"

"Wasn't it?" He looked tired suddenly, drawn in upon himself and older. "I'm sorry you didn't think so. Come and tell me why."

"No!" She resisted his attempt to draw her aside. Panic was all at once loose in her, a wild, unreasoning wash of uncontrollable feeling jangling and jumbled up so that she could not any longer pretend to be in command of it. She pulled away from him, freed her hand from his tight clasp and rushed past him out of the door, her one thought to get away, to escape from all the staring eyes, the politely astonished and secretly avid faces, and to be alone.

The street was an unreal world of warm, purple

sky, the glow of lamps, the gleam and movement of passing traffic. A taxi cruised by, its 'for hire' sign lit up. She hailed it, and in a moment more was safely enclosed by the dark cab and moving away from Charles Langton, out of his life again as abruptly as she had re-entered it. It was best—really it was for the best. But knowing that it was so could not stop the tears that blinded and choked her. All in a few moments her peace of mind and her security had been shattered. They would not so easily be put together again this time.

Twelve

She had got her key in the lock of the heavy front door in Blisham Square when a hand fell on her shoulder. She whirled round, her first instinct to lash out in self-defence, but he caught her wrist and held it, and in the light from a street lamp she saw him smile.

"Not so fast," he said. "I'm not letting you get away this time without a proper explanation."

"Charles!" Her legs were like water under her, and she leaned against the door for support, her throat closed up, her eyes still smarting from the recent tears.

"Invite me in," he demanded.

"No. Charles, no, it isn't any good. I wish you'd just go away and leave me alone."

"Oh, I shan't do that. If you don't invite me in I shall stand here and create the most fearful scene, and the neighbours will all complain and you'll be thrown out into the street."

His tone was light, but he was only half joking; she believed that if she were to deny him he would do just as he threatened, or worse. Beneath the teasing lay determination and anger, and neither was so very far from the surface.

"Let me go, then, or I can't unlock the door," she said. He did so, but he kept a hand on her arm and she could not have got through the door without him.

The light was on in the white painted hall.

"I live at the top," she said. "It's a long way up."

"You think that might deter me? I assure you it won't."

But her own legs felt unequal to the climb. It took every ounce of will-power she possessed to get up the long flights of stairs to the attic floor, and there her hand shook so violently when she tried to open her door that he had to take the key from her and open it himself.

She switched on the lights. Across the room, in the shiny glass of the further wall, reflections moved; Charles Langton and herself, looking just like any couple returned home after an evening out. She hurried to blot them out, drawing the long, heavy blue curtains and switching on a standard lamp to dispel the chill look of the bare, long room.

Charles came a little way forward, looking about him, his face betraying nothing of what he might be thinking. He was wearing a dinner jacket and black tie, and looked withdrawn and formidable, increasing her feelings of defensiveness; she felt that she ought to apologise for the bareness of the room, for its lack of elegance, the shabbiness of its furnishings. Instead, she turned to him and said, "You got here very quickly."

"I took the next cab and told him to follow you. He assumed that I was a private detective—I rather enjoyed it."

"But you could have found me tomorrow. Through Nicholas Behr, I mean."

"I didn't want to wait until tomorrow."

"Oh." Desperately she cast about in her mind for something else to say, something light and uncaring to put off the moment of confrontation. But he did not allow it. He came forward and took her hand, drawing her to sit beside him on the cushioned divan.

"We have a lot to talk about," he said.

"Have we?" She could not look at him. But he put a hand beneath her chin and tilted her face until her eyes at last reluctantly met his, and she could evade him no longer. Then he smiled, a little, crooked smile.

"You know," he said, "it's not like you to run away. Or at least it's not like the person I thought you were. Maybe I was wrong. But I have to be sure. It can't be left in the air, can it?"

"I don't know what sort of person you thought I was."

"Straightforward. Not at all the sort of girl to go back on everything she had said in the space of an afternoon—not without some very compelling reason."

A moment's heavy silence lay between them. Tathwell, thought Jenny; it all came back to that wretched afternoon—to Amelia and his mother and what she had overheard them saying. But she did not know how to begin to tell him, or even whether she could tell him and make him understand what they had meant to her, those cold and careless words.

"Perhaps you accepted defeat too easily," he said at last. "Or perhaps you thought it wasn't worth the fight."

"I don't understand you."

"My mother, I mean, and Amelia. Not that they admit to anything, of course, but clearly there must have been something, some incident more than I was aware of, that day at Tathwell."

The silence this time was very long, and in it she could hear the sound of her own heart beating and the unevenness of her own breathing, and in the background the restless, dim, unceasing roar of the city's life going on all around them, enclosing them in their own small pocket of stillness.

She laced her thin fingers together to keep them from trembling, and looked down at them, struggling for the right words.

"It wasn't much," she said at last. "At least, looking back it doesn't seem like much to have frightened me so. But at the time it felt—dreadful. I overheard them, you see. I was waiting on the terrace for you and Rowena to come out, and I heard your mother and Amelia talking about me—and about you. And even then it wasn't so much what they said as their way of saying it—so worldly, so— oh, they made the gulf between my assumptions and theirs seem a thousand miles wide! They spoke as if I were some girl you'd picked up off the streets and embarrassingly brought home—all very regrettable, but of course one knows that such people do exist and that men—that you—oh, they implied that it was the sort of thing that happened from time to time, though usually you were honest with such creatures—" Her voice had run out of control; she laughed, but it came out as a sob. "They were so loftily tolerant, that was what made me feel really cheap! They even considered me quite pretty, in an anaemic, board-school sort of way!"

He listened in silence.

"I see," he said at last, and there were depths of weariness and pain in his voice. When she dared to look at him she saw eyes dark with anger. "And you believed them," he said. "Of course you believed them."

"Charles, I didn't know what to believe or to think! See it from my point of view—oh, please try to see. It had all been so unreal—the whole summer, the castle, the ball, the car you sent for me; a way of life unlike anything I'd ever known. I felt lost. I couldn't judge, having no secure standpoint left to me, having spent all that time rearranging my ideas—I could only see the picture they were painting, and it was horrible. I didn't want to be in it. So I tried to go on as though nothing had happened, as though you were nothing to me, or rather—oh, you know what I mean!"

"I know that you put me very deliberately at arm's length again, when I had thought myself justified in coming very much nearer. We walked all afternoon and you hardly said a civil or natural word to me; you seemed to have retreated, as if you'd reconsidered and come to the conclusion that—oh, heaven knows! I could make no sense of it. But afterwards there was talk of John Morley, if you remember. And when he came for you, you went to him as if—"

"But he was a friend, a nice, safe friend! Besides, he's always loved Rowena."

"Blind as I am, I didn't know it then. I could only remember that you'd come to the ball with him, that I'd seen you out riding together, that people were talking of what a good thing it would be for Clare, if you were to marry her brother. And then the last time I saw you, you were in his arms."

"But—that was the day I jumped the boundary fence on one of your best horses. Heavens, he was only helping me down!"

"Impressions can be deceptive, can't they, Jenny?"

She was shaken into sudden, sober self-appraisal. Had she not let impressions influence her too strongly? Instead of following the truth she had sensed in him, she had allowed a distorted and fanciful picture to grow in her head until it had engulfed common sense. She had listened to his mother and Amelia and had permitted their waspishly spoken words to colour her whole image of him and of what he might feel, disregarding all he had said and all she had promised him. Yet it had never occurred to her that the love she felt for him might be less than absolute or strong!

"There's no way I can defend myself," she said

helplessly. "I was a little fool, I see that now. But Charles, imagine how it seemed t me! I was so naïve—and, oh, such a howling awful snob! Yes, really—I must have been, mustn't I? Or why should it have upset me so much to be treated like the kitchen maid by your mother? But it did hurt, and I hated it—and you didn't seem at all willing to defend me, you wouldn't take my side. I felt so alone."

"You seemed to be managing extraordinarily well."

"It didn't feel like that."

"I'm sorry, Jenny. I ought to have understood. But you appeared so cool, so much in possession of yourself. And knowing your independent spirit, as I thought—" He smiled. "I judged you well able to take care of yourself. Besides, my mother was so busy putting herself hopelessly in the wrong, I didn't want to stop her. I meant, you see, to allow her enough rope to hang herself. She would have been quite without defence after such a performance. She is very much easier to handle when she knows she has behaved atrociously, and I meant to make my stand then, when I could justifiably accuse her of having behaved like a scullery maid herself. D'you see?"

"Ye-es." She shook her head, understanding only dimly, unable to picture to herself the kind of relationship between mother and son that made necessary such maneuvering. "I can't say that I think it's a nice way of going about things."

"But then Mama isn't a nice woman. She's thoroughly spoiled, and I can't change her. She has been used to having her own way all her life, and I have to manage her as she is, not as I wish she were. Besides, Jenny, she's getting old. She learned a world very different from ours and she can't adapt. One has to remember it and forgive her just a little."

"Have things really changed all that much in the circles in which you move?" She shivered suddenly, remembering how the air of Langton had seemed saturated with feudalism, cloven by the great division between The Family and the rest. "I've always lived in the other world, you see," she said. "On the other side of the gulf, so I know how deep it goes. It is real, Charles. My world is different in manners, in morals, even in accent and appearance—"

"Pretty superficial, I would have thought."

"But they all matter!"

"To whom? Have I criticised your manners, your morals, your accent or appearance? And are we considering their relevance to anyone else? By heaven, the one thing I will not give up to anyone is my right to choose, and if I choose you, then there's an end to the matter! The rest of my family and friends must accept it."

"But would they? Charles, would they?"

For a long moment he looked at her, and she saw the anger in his eyes dissolved into a great desolation.

"Does it really matter so much to you?" he asked her. "Does it matter more than I do?"

"Oh no, no!" Blindly then she reached out to him, reached out for the only certainty she knew. His arms closed round her, and they were warm and comforting and strong, making a nonsense of words. She had no argument against him. Pressing her head against his shoulder, hiding her face from him, she said, "Please, Charles, don't let me go again. I destroy myself with argument. I'm not safe, I want to fight every battle before it's begun, I'm so afraid of not winning!"

"Poor Jenny! Too many battles to fight, and half of them imaginary." There was laughter now in his voice, but still she could not look at him.

"I'm a fool," she said, muffled. "That's the real reason you ought to stay away from me. But I love you so much. Really I do, though I know it doesn't seem like it, the way I've behaved. And I know it's unreasonable of me to want you, but I can't help it. I tried to stop myself—"

"Because you thought me out of reach."

"Yes. The Cinderella feeling."

"But she did marry her prince in the end," he pointed out. "I only hope that, having married him, she managed not to drive him mad by being eternally grateful to him for his condescension. I'll have none of that from you, you know. No feudalism, no Cophetua and the beggar maid. You take me as an equal or not at all."

She turned her head then and looked up at him. Amusement lifted a corner of his mouth and lurked in the grey eyes, but there was determination behind the teasing, and a deep and desperate seriousness.

"I love you, Jenny," he said. "I want to marry you. I

know it's not reasonable after so short a time, when we hardly know one another, yet it seems to me that already I know what most matters about you. And besides, a marriage is made afterwards through the years, it doesn't happen all at once. The most one can be sure of is, here is a person I could build a marriage with, a person I want to spend the rest of my life getting to know; a person who looks at life in a way I respect and like. Is that what you mean when you say that you love me?"

"Oh, yes—that, and—"

"This?" he suggested, and touched her lips with his in the gentlest, most tender of kisses.

It was the ultimate argument. Suddenly it was the only thing that really mattered, and all the rest paled into irrelevance beside her need for him, her utter conviction of belonging to him in this way.

"You might have done it sooner," she murmured against his lips. "It would have saved such a waste of words."

"You think I should have swept you into my arms in front of a whole gallery of art fanciers?"

"It would have been rather nice. Oh, Charles—" Suddenly she remembered, and pushed herself away from him, aghast. "Your mother! What did you do with her when you came after me? You can't just have left her standing there—"

"Can't I?" He grinned. "As a matter of fact that's exactly what I did. I turned tail and fled the gallery, leaving her to her own devices. For all I know she's still there, though I've no doubt she'll find her own way home quite efficiently. Does it matter?"

"Of course it matters! You left her for me. It's symbolic, isn't it?"

"Darling, darling!" Laughing, he folded her in his arms again, rocking her against him as if she were a child. "Truly, I left the nursery long ago. You needn't ever worry about that again. Look—later we'll go and see her, dispose for ever of this terrible ogre you're so afraid of. But for the moment, forget her. Do you think I can make you forget her?"

He had no need to ask, but only to kiss her, and then kiss her again until there was nothing left in the world but themselves and the urgency of their love. And so it was very much later when at last they went out into the world again and walked the short distance between Blisham and Milton Squares.

The house was very much as Jenny had pictured it inside. It was strange to find herself standing in the hall she had so many times, despite herself, imagined, surrounded by that indefinable hush which belongs only to the houses of the very rich. There were thick carpets underfoot, and on the silky, dull crimson walls hung pictures that would have made Daddy Behr's fingers itch.

The Countess had a sitting-room upstairs. All the way up, Charles kept a reassuring hand on Jenny's arm, but she felt no fear. She was sure enough of him now to be able to face anything, and any misgivings that troubled her were on the Dowager's behalf rather than on her own. She waited quite calmly as he knocked gently on his mother's door, and when a voice bade them enter she went serenely into the room.

The Countess reclined on a couch in the centre of a room that was all dim, silvery pastel colours. There seemed to Jenny to be tables everywhere, covered with a great clutter of photographs and painted miniatures and little ornaments. There was a smell of pot-pourri and a suggestion of silks and flutter and femininity, but after the style and taste of half a century ago.

"Charles, darling!" the Countess greeted him petulantly. "Too bad of you to run away like that and leave me! What *were* you thinking of? Really, that wretched little man who owns the gallery simply walked me off my feet, and all I wanted was to see Rowena's portrait. By the time we got to it I hardly had strength to stand and look at it."

"Mama, forgive me. It was naughty of me to desert you, I know, but you see I had to talk to Jenny."

"Oh." For the first time the Countess looked directly at Jenny. There was no warmth or favour in the look, but neither was there open hostility. Jenny decided that the next move must be hers.

"I'm sorry to have taken him away from you," she said. "But I didn't realise that he was going to rush off and leave you like that."

"I hope that you'll see he doesn't make a habit of it. A man who has no time for his mother is usually a thoroughly inconsiderate creature to live with."

And that, thought Jenny, was the nearest thing to acceptance she could hope for yet.

"If you would ring for Marshall," the Countess went on, "I daresay we might have some kind of a nightcap. It's very late."

Elaine Daniel

Charles did as he was bidden. Jenny, watching him, saw that a smile lurked about the mobile corners of his mouth. Affection welled through her and made her reckless.

"It was a lovely portrait of Rowena," she said. "I'm glad she's going to marry John Morley. He's so very much in love with her."

"Headlong marriages seem to be the fashion," grumbled the Countess. "No sense of propriety or form, no predictability any more. The modern way is quite beyond my understanding."

"We must get them safely married," said Charles deliberately, "and then we can begin to think about our own wedding. At Langton, I hope, Jenny?"

"Oh, of course. How could it be anywhere else?"

"And I'm sure the Morleys would want you to be married from their house. Clare will be thrilled to bits."

"I have such a conscience about her, Charles. Are she and Edward and all the rest quite well?"

"Flourishing—groaning under the weight of weddings, but enjoying every moment. And of course, next week is the end of the season, time for the Corn Ball."

"I'd forgotten!" And suddenly a wave of nostalgia, of longing for the place came over her, as if it were home and she an exile of many years.

"You'll come, of course?" he said.

"If Daddy Behr will let me. I'd have to take time off."

"Nonsense," said the Countess crisply and unexpectedly. "If you are going to marry my son, as I understand you are, then you cannot go on working for that man. It isn't suitable. Charles, you will speak to him and arrange everything."

"Of course, Mama," he said soothingly, and grinned at Jenny, who understood that she was being taken in hand. It was, she thought, the only line left for the Countess to take. And up to a point she would permit it, because until some kind of a working relationship had been established it was her only line too. There would be Charles to see that it did not get out of hand. From now on, Charles would always be there when she wanted him.

Her homecoming to Langton was perfect. The trees there were still on fire with autumnal splendour, and the castle crowned its hill with gold in the mellow sunlight. At Morleys, kindness and delight wrapped her round so that she felt she could never be insecure again.

"It was terrible to have lost you," Clare told her, "but in an odd way, you know, it helped things along. There had been so much talk about you and John, you see—people were sure there was a romance, and I suppose the Dowager must have fostered that impression, because one day when he and John were talking the Earl asked straight out what had gone wrong. And John couldn't think of anything to do but tell him the truth, including about him and Rowena, and I suppose a bit about how you'd felt. So Charles dashed straight off to look for you."

"Clare, will you ever forgive me for not letting

you know where I was? I asked my mother not to forward letters or let anyone know, I was so anxious to hide myself. But it was horribly selfish."

"Sometimes one has the right to be selfish," said Clare. "Besides. it's all come out right now, hasn't it?"

And it had. Dancing in Charles' arms under the dazzling chandeliers in the ballroom of Langton Castle, Jenny felt that everything fulfilled the promise of that night in spring when she had first danced with him there. The flowers now were rich with the fullness of autumn, the pillars and arches wreathed with corn, the alcoves piled with fruit. Everything breathed and glowed ripeness, as if the time and the place had wrought their own magic and brought about this conclusion. All about them the ballroom and the people whirled, but at the heart of everything, enclosing them, was the stillness of their own private world.

"Happy, Cinderella?" he murmured against her ear as they danced.

"Happy," she assured him.

"But this time no midnight. Promise?"

"No midnight," she promised him, and knew that there never would be again.

ABOUT THE AUTHOR

Elaine Daniel lives in Spilsbury, Lincolnshire with her two daughters. She attended Durham University and has a BA in English. Her hobbies are local history and photography, also cats of which she has four. She loves the theatre, particularly ballet and opera. She has held many jobs including student of opera at Covent Garden, office temp, verbatim reporter, photographer and teacher. She writes all her novels in longhand.

CIRCLE OF LOVE

Step out of your world and enter the Circle of Love.

Six new CIRCLE OF LOVE romances are available every month. Here's a preview of the six newest titles, on sale April 15, 1982:

☐ **THE BOTTICELLI MAN** by Alexandra Blakelee (#21515-9 • $1.75)

Young American art student Ursula Stewart stood before Count Enrico Benvoglio in the dazzling Roman sunshine. He opened the door of his chauffeured black Mercedes and whisked her off into the velvet Italian night. His resemblance to a fifteenth-century Botticelli masterpiece was uncanny! But Ursula soon discovered that Enrico was very much a twentieth-century man—and too dangerously seductive for any woman to trust.

☐ **VOICES OF LOVING** by Anne Neville (#21538-8 • $1.75)

Jane Murray fell in love with Max Carstairs the first time she saw the famed actor. But soon tragedy drove Max into a reclusive new identity as a mystery writer. Now, unbelievably, Jane was Max's private secretary, winning his trust, igniting his passion. But she hadn't counted on Margot Copeland, a dazzling, dangerous rival, who would stop at nothing to steal Max's love.

☐ **LOVE'S DREAM** by Christine West (#21514-0 • $1.75)

Sharon's job took her far away from the civilized Australian seacoast to a cattle station in the vast Outback—and to Nat, who tantalized her, yet seemed forever beyond her grasp. Like the land itself, Nat was harsh, overbearing and implacable, challenging Sharon to tame his dauntless spirit and claim her place in his wild heart.